TAKE ME DOWN

RIGGS BROTHERS, BOOK 2

JULIE KRISS

ISBN: 978-1-989121-00-9

Also in the Riggs Brothers series: Drive Me Wild

Created with Vellum

ONE

Jace

THIS PARTY WAS like a hundred others. The music was loud, the beer was warm, and the partygoers were well on their way to pissed. By the time I stepped out of the back door of the house and into the yard to catch some air—and maybe some silence—I felt like I could have gone back in time to the wild, drunken parties I'd been to when I was eighteen.

Except now I was twenty-five, dead fucking sober, and I'd just gotten out of prison.

I pulled my leather jacket on, since I'd taken it off in the heat of the party inside, and took a breath. A man and a woman were out here, huddled together and talking intimately as the woman smoked a cigarette. When they saw me, they went quiet and the woman put her cigarette out. They went back into the party, both of them giving me a wide berth.

I was used to it. I was over six feet tall, bearded, leather-jacketed, and an ex-con—most people gave me a wide berth. That was fine with me because it left the back deck as all mine. Inhaling the smell of leftover cigarette smoke, I sat on the step and looked out over the yard and the woods beyond, wishing I'd brought a book with me.

The door behind me opened, and Patrick—the homeowner and party-thrower—dropped down on the step next to me. "Brought you a beer," he said, handing it to me.

"Solo cup?" I asked, looking at the drink in my hand.

He shrugged. "It's a kegger, man. Tradition."

I put the cup down on the step next to me.

"You should drink it," Patrick said. "That's what the party's for."

"It's hot as piss."

"Maybe, but it'll get you wasted."

"When have you ever seen me wasted?"

He had to think about that. I'd known—*been acquainted with* was the better term—Patrick since high school, and he'd been to plenty of those wild parties years ago. I was there, but I was never the one getting shitfaced. I was the quiet Riggs brother, the solitary one, whereas my three brothers were the rowdy bad boys.

"Okay, never," Patrick admitted, "but maybe you should try it. This is your getting out of jail party, after all."

I shot him an amused look. "You were planning to throw this kegger anyway."

"Yeah, but when I found out you were back in town, I decided it was in your honor."

I shook my head. A few weeks ago I'd left the mandatory halfway house in Detroit and moved back to my hometown of Westlake, Michigan. Twenty months—I'd been twenty months in prison, and it felt like it five years. Patrick was probably right that I should cut loose for once in my life, but that probably wasn't going to happen. The beer really was warm. Besides, if my parole officer caught wind of it I'd be in trouble again. I was supposed to walk the straight and narrow with no exceptions—something people who haven't been to prison never think about.

Next to me, Patrick drained his own Solo cup. "Okay, I scoped it out for you," he said. "Janelle or Nika are my picks. I think they're good to go."

I looked at him. "What?"

He blinked half-drunkenly at me. "To fuck," he said clearly. "Either one of them is down to fuck. You just got out of prison, man. Don't tell me you don't want some pussy."

I searched my brain. There had been a few introductions while I was inside at the party, trying to act normal. Janelle was a blonde, pretty except for the exhausted bags under her eyes and the fact that she was too thin. Nika had a big tangle of curly hair and was wearing a black T-shirt with the words emblazoned across her breasts in glitter: NO TIME FOR FUCKBOYZ. I honestly had no idea what that meant and wasn't sure I would meet her standards.

"I'm good, thanks," I said.

Patrick nodded. "I get it. You're a Riggs. Everyone knows you guys. I mean, we always knew your brothers cleaned up like nobody's business. You probably get more than you can handle."

This was so off-base that I almost laughed. Not five minutes ago, a woman had crept past me like she thought I would mug her. "You have got to be fucking kidding me."

"I'm just saying." Patrick held up his hands, not finished giving me his philosophy. "This is a celebration. A guy gets out of prison, he should get maximum pussy. Like an endless string. This is a good party, and the rooms upstairs are empty. At least get your dick sucked. I think Janelle was checking you out."

She had checked me out. I was intimidating, but I was also noticeable. I was six-three, and I'd done pushups and situps for twenty months to keep myself sane. I wasn't bulked, but I was hard as a fucking rock, which was not an accident. Still, that didn't mean I wanted my dick sucked.

Well, I did. Of course I fucking did. I was twenty-five and I wanted to get laid. But not here. Not tonight. Not from her.

Apparently, not ever.

Twenty-five, and it was the story of my fucking life.

"Thanks for the idea, but I'm not going to get that girl to blow me," I said.

Patrick laughed. "Are you a Riggs or what?"

I knew what he meant. My brothers and I were the notorious bad boys of Westlake. We were born on the wrong side of the tracks, and our mothers had taken off early on. That left us with our father, who had let us run wild. My brothers—Luke, Ryan, and Dex—were good-looking, charismatic in different ways, and pretty irresistible to women. Luke had landed Emily Parker, a cop's daughter and gorgeous blonde. Ryan was a baseball player who had to beat women off with a stick. And in high school Dex had thrown a party where every girl in attendance was required to be topless. *Required.* And dozens of them had done it. That party had gone down as one of the rowdiest in Westlake's history; the cops got called six times.

I'd been part of all that, but I was on the sidelines. I was Jace Riggs, the quiet one, the one who tended to walk the straight and narrow. Until I'd surprised everyone by going to prison for stealing cars.

So yeah, I was a Riggs after all.

"Let me ask you something," I said to Patrick now. "Don't you ever want a woman you can talk to?"

His drunk look of bafflement was almost funny. "What?"

"Talk," I said. "Like two people, instead of a girl and a guy who's trying to get her to blow him."

"I try to get every girl to blow me," Patrick said, as if this were obvious. "Don't you?"

I rubbed my fingertips over the beard on my jaw. "In the land of the blind, the one-eyed man is king."

Now he was completely lost. "What?"

"Nothing." I stood up. "Thanks for the party, man. I've gotta go."

It was late August, and the air smelled unbearably sweet after the stink of the house. Twenty months in a cell meant I would never take fresh air for granted again. I let my mind drift as I walked down the drive and the street toward Melcroft Road, where there was a bus stop. I had no car, though Luke said he would get me a junker from the body shop. That sounded good, but in the meantime taking the bus had become second nature.

It was late. I was headed back to the house where I grew up, where Luke lived now. There was a guest house behind the house, which made us sound rich when we were the opposite. The guest house was a leftover from when the house had belonged to someone wealthy a hundred years ago, but right now it was mine, rent-free.

And that all sounded good, except that as always, I was alone.

I should do something about that, but at the moment I didn't know what.

Well, I thought as the bus pulled up, if I wanted to talk to someone, I'd be doing it tomorrow. Except it wouldn't be a woman. I had a court-mandated appointment with a counselor, a guy named John White who was supposed to help me adjust to post-prison life. Or something. I wasn't looking forward to it, but I'd already lived at the halfway house until I was allowed to leave, getting random drug checks from my parole officer, even though I'd never had a drug problem. Anything to get the system off my back, I'd do.

Whether John White knew the real truth about me and the time I'd done, the thing that no one else knew, I had no idea. I guessed I'd find out.

There was only one other person on the bus, a young woman in a polyester uniform, coming home from a shift somewhere. I took a seat by the window and unwound my earbuds from my pocket, plugging them into my phone and putting them in my ears. She still got up and moved all the way to the back, as far from me as she could go.

I couldn't blame her. It was past midnight, we were alone, and I looked like trouble. She couldn't take chances. She had to be smart.

Still, I turned up the music, looked out the window, and made myself think about nothing at all.

TWO

Tara

"JACE RIGGS IS YOURS."

The file landed on the desk in front of me with a slap. I looked up and saw my colleague and boss, John White, turning to leave my office already.

"What?" I asked. "Where are you going?"

"Home," he said. "My daughter has the flu."

I checked the clock. A quarter to one. "Is he one o'clock?" I asked in a panic.

John waved a hand over his shoulder. "You didn't have a one o'clock anyway. I checked."

He was still walking, so I got up, moved around my desk, and followed him. "I don't know him," I said.

"Neither do I."

"What am I trying to do here?"

"The usual. Read the file."

"I have fifteen minutes, John," I said. "Give me the rundown."

We were across the hall in his office now, and he sighed as he looked around for his keys. "Riggs," he said. "The name mean anything to you?"

"No. Should it?"

He smiled at me. He was a decent guy in a not-too-expensive suit, going home to his sick kid. "I thought you'd lived in Westlake all your life."

"I moved here when I was ten."

"Then you should know the Riggs family. Everyone does. They live in that property on Welmer, on the other side of the tracks."

I knew it. It was a big plot with a big house on it, but it was run-down. Probably someone rich had built the place, but now it was a mess with weeds in the yard, in a part of town no one went to if they could help it.

"Mike Riggs has four sons," John said. "Not all from one woman, as I recall. In any case, the women left years ago. The sons are all trouble. Mike himself is currently incarcerated for vehicular attempted murder. That is, he tried to run someone over in his car while they were having a drunken argument."

I winced. "Ouch."

"While Mike's been inside, it's also come out that he was running a stolen car business through the body shop he owns, Riggs Auto. The whole thing is being dismantled by the Westlake PD, so Mike Riggs is not going to walk free anytime soon. You're about to see one of his sons. Birth name John Christian, which is shortened to J. C., which in turn is shortened to Jace. It's all anyone has ever called him. He just did twenty months for grand theft auto."

"Okay," I said, feeling a little deflated already. It was always hardest to work with someone who was following a family pattern. "Like father, like son."

"Probably," John said. He had found his keys and we left his office so he could lock the door. "Jace is twenty-five, no priors, no violent history. Drug and alcohol tests have all come in clean. His PO says that when he did random checks at the halfway house, he usually found the kid reading a book. He says if Jace was putting him on, it was pretty convincing."

"People read books," I argued.

"Guys like Jace Riggs don't read books," John said. "What you're doing is a court-mandated session to make sure he's adjusting to civilian life. Talk to him for an hour, write something in the file, and move on."

"And if he's not adjusting?" I asked.

"Then see him two or three times, write something in the file, and move on," John said. "You know how it goes, Tara. You've been doing this for a while now. I have to go."

I stood in the hallway after he left. He was right, I'd been doing this for a while, though it didn't feel like long to me. I was still the junior counselor here because I'd only graduated three years ago. John ran an office of psychiatrists and psychologists that took a mix of paying clients and court-mandated cases. The paying clients were more profitable, but John said he believed in not only making money but helping people who had been pushed, as he put it, to the bottom of the pile.

It was kind of him, but it didn't stop him from taking the top clients for himself and leaving the bottom of the pile to me.

Not that I saw Jace Riggs as beneath me. I didn't. One of the reasons I became a licensed psychological counselor was because I believed that everyone, even people who had done wrong, deserved to get help if they needed it. But John was right, this was a routine case. All I had to do was ask Jace Riggs a few questions, let him talk for an hour, and put his file away forever.

Still, I leafed through the file as I waited for him to show up. It was surprisingly thin. Aside from his family life, Jace Riggs wasn't the kind of guy who went to prison. No juvenile record, no addiction, no history of abuse. If he hadn't started stealing cars, he wouldn't be in the system at all.

I was pondering that, curious, when the door opened and he walked in.

I had been ready for a lot of things in my life. Ready to move out, away from my parents. Ready to end my long-term relationship with Kyle, my last boyfriend and the guy I almost married. Ready to start this career and work hard at it, no matter what it took.

I was not ready for Jace Riggs.

THREE

Tara

HE WAS BIG, over six feet. Long, muscled legs in worn jeans. Motorcycle boots. A gray T-shirt and a worn black leather jacket that fit him like a glove. Dark hair cut neatly, a little shorter at the sides and longer on top. Dark, trim beard. High cheekbones, gray eyes with dark lashes. He looked at me from those eyes as he leaned a little over the desk and held his hand out. "Hey," he said. "I'm Jace."

He was good-looking, sure, but not the kind of guy who could be a model. He was too rough for that. He looked like a thug, like a car thief, a con. He wasn't bulky like a football player, but seeing him head-on, my eyes trying not to crawl the flat stomach above his silver belt buckle, I couldn't help but notice he was absolutely one hundred percent muscle, like a man who could knock you over with one blow.

But it was his eyes that caught me. They were calm, intelligent, deep with thought. A little sad, maybe. Eyes that had seen things. Eyes that were, right now, seeing me.

I cleared my throat and said, "Hi. I'm Tara. I'm, er, John's replacement."

"They told me." He shook my hand. He wore three silver rings, one on his fourth finger, one on his middle, and a thin silver circlet on his thumb. I felt them brush my skin before he pulled away,

He sat in the chair across from me, slouched back just a little the way big guys do. I looked at the line of his thigh, the line of his shoulders in the jacket. I looked at his mouth, framed by the short beard. *Holy hell.* I was having a visceral reaction to this man, and it had to stop now.

"I think you know," I said, resisting the urge to fidget with the papers and pens on my desk, "that this is a court-mandated follow-up visit. To discuss how you've been doing since your release."

"Yeah," Jace Riggs said. "I know."

"We can talk about your life since you left the halfway house," I said. "How has it been, Jace? How do you feel you're adjusting?"

He looked at me for a long moment. I wondered what he saw. A nice enough looking woman, I supposed. I was twenty-seven, and I'd twisted my brown hair at the back of my neck. I dressed carefully for this job—too formal, and my clients saw me as unfriendly, too casual and they didn't take me seriously. I compromised today with dark jeans, ankle boots, and a silk shell top with a casual blazer over it. The silk shell was feminine and would be revealing on most women, but my breasts were so small I could wear it without them spilling out.

So that was my look: competent counselor with small boobs. Some of the men I worked with tried to check them out, as if they could inflate them by staring. Jace Riggs didn't seem to notice.

I couldn't read his expression, but he tilted his head, just a tiny fraction, as if he was waiting for me to say something.

I was quiet. One of the first rules of counseling is that you can let quiet happen. The counselor should never talk just to fill the void. Filling the void is the client's role, not yours.

Still, Jace looked almost expectant. Then he said, "I'm adjusting fine, I guess."

"Are you employed?" I asked.

He frowned, a graceful turn of his mouth as he watched me. "Isn't that in your file?"

"No. Nothing since your last parole officer report, in the halfway house in Detroit, is here in your file." I tried giving him a friendly smile. "That's why we're here to talk."

"Hmm." He lifted a hand and rubbed his index finger along his lower lip. He had remarkable hands, large and full of masculine grace, the fingers long and capable. His rings were very male and not showy, silver bands stamped with patterns, the narrow circle on his thumb. The skin at the base of his thumb had a smear of black on it—motor oil.

"Is something wrong?" I asked him, to cover the fact that I was slowly getting turned on by looking at his hand.

He stopped rubbing his lip. "To be honest, I'm trying to figure out what you want me to say."

That surprised me, and I raised my gaze to his face. "I want you to say the truth."

Amusement rippled across his eyes. They were like a calm ocean, those eyes, gray and beautiful yet deeply alive. And his lashes were ridiculous. Good god, I needed to get a grip.

He waited another moment—this was one client who was fine with letting the quiet happen—as if he thought I might say something more, and then he said, "I'm working at my family's auto body shop."

The one his father had run, that had stolen cars moving through it. "I see," I said.

"You think I'm still dealing in stolen cars," Jace said, reading my mind. "I'm not. My brother Luke and I have taken over the shop with Dad in prison. We reopened it and we're running it our own way. The legal way. Where we make money by actually fixing cars."

"Do you get along with your brother?" I asked.

Jace laughed softly, and I stilled in fascination at the sound. *The sons are all trouble,* John had said. "Luke and I haven't killed each other," he said. "I suppose you can call that getting along."

"So you fight?"

"We bloodied each other's noses plenty as kids," Jace said. "We keep it more civil now."

"I see. There's some tension, then."

He tilted his chin again, that tiny movement I only saw because I was watching him so closely. "You're asking because you think I have family issues that affect my patterns and my behavior."

I was doing that. *Exactly* that. So of course I said, "I'm not doing anything. I'm only asking how you're doing."

"Do you get along with your siblings?" he asked me.

I opened my mouth, and so help me God, the words almost came out: *I'm an only child, and I haven't seen my parents in months.* That was how easily he could trap me. I backtracked and gave the right answer instead. "We aren't here to discuss me. However, in your case it's quite possible that your father instilled behavior in you from an early age that makes you—"

"I think you're an only child," he said.

Jesus, was he psychic or just uncannily observant? How could he even know? I ran my fingers along the edges of the file on my desk. "Mr. Riggs—"

"I'm Mr. Riggs now." Amused.

"Jace." I emphasized the word to show I wasn't afraid of him. "What you're doing may seem clever to you, but in fact it's a very common tactic. I've seen it many times before."

"What tactic?" he said. "I find you interesting."

Another hit. It was like he was shooting arrows from the other side of my desk, sending them straight through my armor. Because people found me nice. They found me competent. A few of them even found me attractive. But the fact was, no one found me interesting. No one except Jace Riggs. If he was telling the truth, that was.

"The tactic," I said clearly, "is deflection. Sending the questions back in my direction. It's a defense mechanism, Jace. Because you don't want to talk about yourself. Because it's too painful."

"It isn't painful to talk about me," he said, annoyance flaring in his voice and his expression. I'd scored my own hit. "It's fucking boring to talk about me. I fix cars, I come to bullshit appointments like this, I do whatever my PO tells me to do. That's all I do. I don't drink, I don't fuck, I don't snort coke up my nose, and I don't have father issues. Whatever little boxes you need to check in that file, you can't check a single one."

I glared at him. I was torn between annoyance—John and I had almost literally talked about which boxes to check in the file before Jace came to this appointment—and a sort of weird fascination, mixed with lurid curiosity at the words *I don't fuck*. What did that mean? He was celibate for some reason? Heartbreak, or sexual dysfunction, or something else? Was he into men? *Please, God, let him not be into men. Though that would be admittedly hot. But still.*

"Okay then," I said, because I'm a terrible person and the curiosity about his sex life won. It totally fucking won. "Let's backtrack. You mentioned your personal life. Where are you living now that you're in Westlake?"

Jace rolled his eyes. "I'm living in the guest house at the family place while my brother and his girlfriend live in the main house. Still not interesting, doc."

"I'm not a doctor," I corrected him. "I'm licensed to practice, but I don't have a medical license. I can't prescribe."

"I told you, I'm not doing drugs. I'm not here looking for Lorazepam or Oxy."

How had this conversation gone so far off the rails? "It sounds like you have a stable living situation," I said, trying to act like the counselor I was supposed to be. "How about your social situation? You've lived in Westlake all your life. Do you have a circle of friends for support?"

His gray eyes went a little hard at that. "I don't have friends," he said. "My brothers and I have never had friends. Everyone in Westlake has always thought we're scum, and they still think it."

"Surely that's an exaggeration," I said, thinking of John saying *the sons are all trouble*, like he knew perfectly well. "People aren't as judgmental as you think."

"Yes, they are," Jace countered. "Though we never gave anyone very many reasons to befriend us. Dex beat up half the boys in Westlake, Luke beat up the other half, and Ryan screwed all the girls."

I didn't know what to make of that, but we weren't talking about his brothers. "And you?" I asked him. "What did you do?"

"You mean, did I do the beating or the screwing?" Jace shrugged. "It didn't matter what I did. I got the consequences anyway. I'm a Riggs. The truth isn't interesting to anyone when you're a Riggs."

"The truth interests me," I said. "I told you that."

"Fine. What truth do you want? Tell me so I can give it to you and we can get this over with."

I put my hands palm-down on the desk. "I am trying," I said

slowly so I wouldn't scream, "to do my job here. It would help if you were even a little bit cooperative."

He just looked at me, with those ocean-gray eyes. Not promising a yes. Not promising a no. Just waiting for me to come at him.

"Okay," I said, fighting for control of the conversation, like it seemed I had since he walked in the room. "You're not close with your brothers. Your father is obviously not a source of support. You don't have friends. What about romantic relationships? Is there someone in your life?"

It took him a second. His eyes stayed flat and hard at first, and then the penny dropped. His chin tilted up. "Oh, I get it," he said. "That's what you're really asking. You want to know if I'm single."

That was when I did the most unprofessional thing of my career. I jerked my chair back, stood up, and grabbed his file, slamming it on the cabinet behind me.

"That's it," I said. "This session is over."

FOUR

Jace

"YOU DON'T HAVE to do this," I said to my brother. "You know that, right?"

We were standing in the paved yard behind Riggs Auto, a big space bordered by a ratty chain link fence. There were cars here—cars we were working on, cars that didn't run, cars we'd poached for spare parts. There were piles of parts and, like the rest of the place, it stunk of motor oil and tires, spiced with the chemical tang of body paint. I hoped to God that when I died, I did it with that godawful smell in my nose.

My brother Luke shrugged. "I didn't do much. A guy came in and said he inherited this car when his dad died. He didn't want it. I gave him five hundred bucks. It's yours."

I stared at the car between us. It was a Ford Thunderbird, and since my brothers and I knew cars by kindergarten, I knew its distinctive shape: boxy nose, body low to the ground, aluminum wheels, metal trim. It had late 80's written all over it. "The '89 model?" I asked.

"Yeah," Luke said. He was wearing his garage coveralls, like me, though he'd unzipped the top and let it hang, showing his black tee. He was a good-looking piece of shit, my brother Luke. Black hair and dark eyes and muscles and all that stuff. He'd never cleaned up like our brother Ryan—Luke was a bit more reserved with women. Or so we all thought. It turned out that he'd secretly had a relationship with Emily Parker, the cop's daughter, when they were eighteen, and he'd never gotten over her in the years since.

Luke had left town for a while, and so had Emily. Now they were both back, and they'd decided they didn't give a shit what people thought of them being together anymore. Emily lived in the main house with Luke, and had for months now. They were nuts about each other. They tried to be nice about it in public, but it still managed to be annoying as hell.

"Does it run?" I asked Luke as he tossed me the keys over the hood.

"It does," Luke said, "and there's a V6 in there. But it needs a lot of work first. You have your work cut out for you."

Work, I could do. It wasn't a very attractive car—it looked dated—and it was an ugly old-school gray, but I squeezed the keys hard in my hand and tried to look cool about it. I had a car—my own car. I hadn't had one since I'd sold my last one to pay my lawyer's bill when I went to prison because no one needs a car in prison.

"Thanks, man," I said to Luke, trying not to sound like I was emotional or anything.

He shrugged. "It bothered me, seeing you without a car. A Riggs without a car is like a Riggs without a dick."

"I have a dick."

"You do now." He gave me half a grin. "I'm going home to Emily, and if I'm lucky I'll get to use mine. See you later."

I watched him go. He'd get lucky, of course. Now that they were back together, he and Emily were barely able to stay off each other. I never went to the main house, especially unannounced, in case I saw something I couldn't unsee.

My brothers and I weren't close growing up, even though we lived in the same house. That was Dad's fault. He didn't so much raise us as let us through the door every once in a while when it was cold out, like dogs. It was every man for himself in the Riggs house, and Dex, Ryan, Luke, and I grew up mostly fending for ourselves. Dex had been a cop for a while before he burned out of the job. Ryan had been a baseball player on his way up until his bad shoulder and shitty attitude put a stop to his career. They were both in Detroit, as pissed off as ever.

But Luke had changed. After his years away, driving around the country from place to place, he was back in Westlake for good. He was fixing up the house and rebuilding Riggs Auto with me. It had to do with Emily, and it wasn't just about the fact that Luke was getting laid. It was about the fact that he'd found the person who made him want to do all that shit. The woman he was building a life for. The woman who was doing the same for him.

And that made me think of the crazy, disastrous counseling session I'd had three days ago. I'd fucked that up. The first attractive, sober woman I'd talked to since getting out, and I'd made a complete mess of it.

Tara Montgomery. That was the name on the nameplate on her desk. She'd riled me up, she'd made me mad, and she'd made me very fucking horny. She'd done it just by sitting behind a desk and asking me a few questions—a quietly beautiful woman with long brown hair tied at the back of her neck, deep brown eyes under arched brows, an expressive mouth, a slender build, no wedding ring. I should have seen her as just another faceless professional, but something about her said *sex* to me. It had been all I could do not to lean over the desk and explore that mouth myself, see if it tasted as good as it looked.

Sure, I could make jokes about it. I had just got out of prison, my balls were neon blue, and just about anything that breathed would look good to me. That was the joke, right? But it wasn't that. It was *her*. I'd walked away from the women at Patrick's party without a second thought, but Tara Montgomery—with her bullshit questions and her steely vulnerability and her ridiculous desire to help me—made me want to lick the skin of her elegant neck and listen to her moan.

I'd felt like an animal. So of course I'd acted like an asshole.

I felt bad about it now. She really had been trying to help, though I was sure she was also digging for details about my sex life. I'm a jerk, but I'm not stupid. Her interest in me wasn't entirely professional—which had only added gasoline to the flames of that crazy session.

The truth interests me, she'd said. But she didn't know the truth about me. That much, I was sure of.

I scrubbed a hand over my face. I should go back for another session, try again. Act like a rational man this time. Apologize. Hell, maybe even get some help. I had to get her stamp of approval to get the system off my back, anyway—I had to convince her I was adjusting to civilian life. I hadn't done a very good job of that by pissing her off and practically coming on her.

I'd see her one more time, and then it would be over. I'd never see her again, and that was for the best. Because even if she felt the same way I did, a woman like that would never have the time of day for a man like me. Not in real life.

I went into the shop to get my tools. In the meantime, I had a car to work on.

FIVE

Tara

THE DAY JACE RIGGS had his second appointment—because, against all odds, the office told me he was coming to see me again—I woke up close to orgasm.

In my half-awake brain, Jace Riggs was naked in my bed. He was solid muscle, powerful and hard. He was on top of me, his wrists pinning me, his mouth on mine, his tongue in my mouth. I couldn't move, could feel nothing but him, could taste nothing but him. I squirmed my hips, my knees apart, and felt only him.

In my fever dream, he broke the kiss and whispered in my ear: *I'm going to fuck you so deep. I'm going to take your sweet cunt. Tell me you want me to.*

"Yes," I said. "Yes."

He pushed inside me, fucking me, and I knew I was awake now but I didn't care. I pushed my fingers into my panties and came hard in three quick strokes, my hips bucking off the mattress.

In the shower fifteen minutes later, I tried to rationalize it. It wasn't all that uncommon, according to the research, to have sexual thoughts about a client. Therapy could be intense, and it could be raw and emotional. Sexual urges were normal human urges that sometimes came out when things were raw and emotional. In fact, there was a term for it: transference, in which one transfers one's intense emotions onto one's therapist, or in this case onto one's client.

No, even though it had never happened to me before, having these urges wasn't wrong. What mattered was whether one acted on those urges—and I had no intention of doing that. Crossing the line to having sex with a client—even if he was agreeable, which I was pretty sure he wasn't—was unthinkable for a counselor, a complete disgrace to the profession and an easy end to one's career.

So everything was fine. Just fine. What I was experiencing was a fully calm, fully rational, fully scientifically documented experience that would not affect my performance as a professional.

Or I just really, really wanted to fuck Jace Riggs.

I shut the water off and ran a hand over my face. "Shit," I said out loud to no one in my small, lonely apartment. "Just get through this session, Tara. It's an hour of your life. Act like the intelligent woman you are, write your report, and get rid of him. Then you never have to see him again."

That sounded good, so I got dressed, put some makeup on, and went to work. The morning orgasm had made me feel pretty good, actually—*thanks, Jace Riggs*. Though I wasn't supposed to think about that.

I did two morning sessions. I talked to John, whose daughter had now recovered from the flu. I did paperwork. I ate lunch, a grilled eggplant sandwich from the Italian deli down the street. I sat at my desk and answered emails and drank a bottle of water and did everything a normal person would do. And when the door opened and Jace Riggs walked in again, I was just about ready. Just about.

But damn it, he had a huge presence. He was wearing much the same outfit as three days ago—jeans, motorcycle boots, T-shirt—except that it was cool out today, so he had added a hoodie beneath the black leather jacket. The hoodie was unzipped, so I could glimpse his chest and his stomach beneath the tee, and he was wearing those rings. This time I noticed that he had two rings on his left hand, too, as well as a thin leather bracelet on the wrist.

Kryptonite. Fucking kryptonite.

He sat in the chair across from me like he'd done the other day, and I could see from his face that he had the same resolve I did. He was going to be polite today. He was going to be businesslike. This was going to be a textbook session.

"Hello, Jace," I said. "How are you?"

He nodded. I was wearing dark jeans topped with a loose-necked thin summer sweater with a cotton camisole beneath it. His gaze did not travel below my chin.

"I'm fine, thanks," he said. "You?"

"Very well, thank you."

"That's good." He drummed his fingers quickly on the arm of his chair—those long, gorgeous fingers that I was not staring at. "I'm sorry about last time. I was an asshole to you. It won't happen again."

It was honest, and it was surprising. And it was nice. "Thank you," I said. "Apology accepted. And I apologize, too. I was unprofessional."

He shrugged. "I made you mad. I get it."

"Okay, then. So we'll start over."

"That's what I'm here for."

This was going well. Really well. We could do this, him and me. I pulled out his file—I'd retrieved it from the cabinet where I'd slammed it last time—and said, "Let's get started. We'll steer away from personal topics for now. I'd like to talk about your time in prison and your arrest. What led up to you being arrested."

"Sure," Jace said. "I guess we can talk about that."

It didn't matter that the last session had ended terribly, that I'd fantasized about this man naked in my bed, fucking me until I came. I could have an hour-long session with Jace Riggs, and everything would be fine. I was sure of it.

I should have known better.

That was the last time we were civil. After that, it all went to hell.

SIX

Jace

JESUS. How did this happen? How was I fighting with my court-appointed counselor? It was just a simple bullshit session. How did I keep fucking it up?

She was wearing a loose top today, some kind of light knit thing with a neck so wide it dropped almost to her shoulders. Beneath it she wore a navy blue tank top, the straps of which were clearly visible. I could see her collarbones, her clavicle. The line of her neck. Her dark brown hair was tied back again, but there were a few tendrils around her face, framing her cheekbones and her chin.

I drummed my fingers on the arms of my chair because I wanted to reach over and ease the straps of her tank top and the neck of her sweater down over her shoulders. Pull them down, down.

Keep it under control, Riggs.

"Let's talk about your career stealing cars," she said.

"Why?" I asked.

She blinked, looked down at her file. "Well, to be honest, you don't fit the profile. No drugs, no prior offenses, no acts of rage. You seem to have started breaking the law relatively late in life."

"So I should have started sooner?" I asked her. "That would have made more sense to you?"

"Criminal behavior is a pattern," Tara Montgomery said calmly. "It's a learned method of dealing with things, and it most often starts early."

She was going to be a professional today, like she'd promised. I'd promised her, too. But I looked at the curve of her bottom lip and I knew she was capable of something else. Of being someone else. I wondered if she had a man, if she liked to fuck him, if he made her come. Which was none of my fucking business.

"Well, I didn't start early," I told her. "I started late."

"Why?" she asked me. "Why did you start? Did you need money?"

"I had a job and an apartment," I said. "I was fine." It was true. I'd been working as a mechanic, which was the only job I knew. Luckily it's a job someone always needs, somewhere.

"Why, then?" Tara pressed. "Was someone threatening you?"

"Anyone who tries to threaten me can do it with their teeth down their throat." Also true.

But she wasn't done. "Was it the thrill of it, then?"

"If I wanted a thrill, I'd get on a damn roller coaster."

"Why, then?" she said, the barest waver of frustration in her voice. Which said I was getting to her.

"I'll tell you on one condition," I said.

She looked exasperated. "What is it?"

"Tell me something true about yourself."

Her eyes went wide and she stared at me.

"Anything," I told her. "It doesn't have to be embarrassing, or even secret. It just has to be true. You ask me all these questions, and you expect me to give you honesty. Well, I want it from you in return. Just once, before this session is over and we never see each other again."

She seemed to think it over. "Okay," she said. "I have something. I'll tell you."

My heart flipped in my chest. I hadn't actually thought she'd say yes. "Go ahead."

I could tell she was choosing her words, her beautiful brown eyes thoughtful, her soft mouth pressed briefly into a line. "I was engaged to be married eight months ago," she said. "We'd been together for two years. We were planning the wedding when I broke it off."

Now my blood was going crazy in my veins. Excitement that she'd done what I asked. Jealousy over whoever this fucking guy was. Fear that she'd change her mind and clam up. "Did he hurt you?" I asked her.

She looked surprised. "No, never. He was a nice guy."

A nice guy who could go fuck himself. "Did he ignore you? Treat you bad in some way?"

"No, he was fine. I just... I wasn't happy. I knew I couldn't be happy with him. So I left."

I was silent. All I could do was look at her. Picture her with a nice guy, a good-looking guy, going out for dinner, laughing at his jokes. Curling up on the couch with him, watching TV. Kissing him, fucking him, telling him she loved him. Meeting his parents. Putting his ring on her finger.

Nice things, normal things that normal people did. She'd done all of those things. Things I'd never done, and felt like I would never do.

I stared at her and she stared back, meeting my gaze. Her cheeks flushed slowly, hotter and then hotter again. There was everything in the air between us, heavy and burning and unsaid.

She parted her lips, made herself speak. "Your turn," she said softly. "Tell me the truth, Jace. Why did you start stealing cars?"

I didn't drop my gaze from hers. "Because I was good at it," I said.

Her cheeks flushed redder, this time with anger. "That isn't the truth," she said. "It's a lie. I told you something true, and you are *lying* to me."

"What does it matter?" I said, my voice rising just like hers was. "It makes no difference what the reason was. I stole cars because I'm a fucking criminal. You have to get used to that, Tara. That's who I am."

"That's bullshit!" The words came out nearly in a shout. I'd never seen a woman so angry at me before, and it was so hot I could have slammed her on the desk and fucked her right there. "Don't give me your bullshit line! Your woe-is-me, I'm-a-Riggs line! I am trying to figure out why a man who is intelligent and sensitive and kind would steal cars and *fuck up his life!*"

"You don't know me," I said to her. "I'm none of those things. You think you know me because your file says I read books? Well, I do. I fucking do. I read books, and I'm *still* a fuckup. That's how it works with real people in the real world, not profiles. Real people don't make any sense."

She made a sound of frustration, nearly a growl, and slapped her palms down on her desk. "You are so fucking frustrating!" she shouted.

I pushed my chair back. "Write your report," I said. "I came here because I need the court off my back, but you know what? I don't care what you write in it. Write that I'm an asshole who can't get through a simple session."

"You think I won't do it?" she said. "Just try me, Jace Riggs. I can make you do these stupid sessions that you hate so much until you're ninety."

"Do it," I said, standing up. She didn't like looking up at me, so she stood up too, and for the first time I saw all of her, the way her sweater draped over her slim hips, the long slender lines of her legs in their dark jeans. Which was fucking great, because now I could picture those legs wrapped around me. Which they would never be. "I paid my debt," I told her. "I served my time. I lived in the halfway house. I report to my PO. I did every court appearance and every random drug test. There's nothing you can do that will scare me. Have a nice life."

"I will," she said, "because I have plenty of clients who actually cooperate. I feel sorry for whoever gets you next."

I left then. Just walked out. It was for the best.

Because she was right—I was lying. She'd given me honesty like I'd asked, and in return I'd lied to her face.

I was good at stealing cars—that part was true. But that wasn't why I started doing it. I started doing it for revenge.

I should have just told her, but what the hell did it matter? Did I think that if I explained myself she'd see me as something different? As a nice guy? A guy she could actually like? That was never going to happen—*we* were never going to happen. And I couldn't just sit across the desk from her, looking at her, knowing that. For once, I just couldn't.

So I'd fucked it up.

But then again, that was all I knew how to really do.

SEVEN

Tara

I WAS A MESS AFTER THAT. I took a walk down the office hall and stood in the break room, staring at the wall for God knows how long until someone walked through the door behind me, jolting me out of my rage-and-lust stupor. Before whoever it was could ask me questions, I turned and left, walking swiftly to the ladies' room this time and hiding in a stall. I was a professional counselor, and I spent thirty-six minutes—I counted—hiding in a goddamned toilet stall, trying not to cry.

Fucking Jace Riggs.

Fuck him and his chest and his stomach and his hands and his long legs in jeans. Fuck his nice hair and his gorgeous mouth and those fucking eyes that said there was so much more going on in his head than he let on. Fuck his I-give-up attitude and his don't-mess-with-me defenses and his insanely fuckable smarts. Fuck all of it.

I closed my eyes and took deep breaths—really not advisable in a bathroom stall—and when I felt human again, I splashed water on my face and walked calmly back to my office. I didn't have another appointment today; all I had to do was wrap up my paperwork and go home.

I sat at my computer and pulled up Jace's electronic file. I pulled up the form the court was expecting me to fill out. I stared at it for a few minutes, and then I started typing.

I wrote that John Christian Riggs, known as Jace, was adjusting as well as could be expected to post-prison life. I wrote that he had a job, a stable place to live, skills that would keep him employed. I wrote that he was free from the addiction, mental illness, or anger problems that were the most frequent contributors to recidivism—that is, ex-cons ending up back in prison. I wrote that he presented himself in counseling as polite, well-mannered, cooperative, and generally willing to please. I wrote that he had stated no desire to return to his former job of stealing cars, that he seemed to have learned his lesson and paid his debt to society. I recommended that his follow-up be put on a reduction schedule and ended.

I need the court off my back, Jace had said. Maybe I couldn't help him, but there was one thing I could do for him, anyway.

You should help him, you idiot, I told myself as I hit send. *That's supposed to be your fucking job.*

I stood up and took my purse from my desk drawer. Heading out of the office, I popped my head in John's door. "Going home," I said. "Have a nice night."

"Tara," he said, putting a file in his filing cabinet and closing the drawer. "I need to talk to you about something. Close the door behind you."

Surprised, I did.

"Jace Riggs," John said. "You had an appointment today?"

Shit. Had Jace complained about my conduct? Well, if he

had, I'd face it. To say I'd been unprofessional was an understatement. "Yes," I said.

John shook his head. "I told them to tell you."

"Told who what? To tell me what?"

"Reception. We weren't supposed to take any more of his appointments. He's off the roster."

"He is?" I felt a beat of panic, not on my own behalf this time. "Is he in trouble again? Is he being sent somewhere else?"

"No, nothing like that." John neatened his desk and powered off his computer, preparing to go home. "We weren't supposed to have him in the first place. He wasn't supposed to be on the list for counseling at all."

That was baffling. "Why not?"

"Turns out he's a CI," John said. "An important one, in fact."

I stared at him. A CI—a confidential informant. Jace had been an inside informer to the police.

Why did you start stealing cars?

Because I was good at it.

"He was informing on his father's stolen car ring?" I asked John.

"Not just that," he said. "The stolen cars were being run by some bigger criminals—drugs, weapons, that kind of thing. Apparently, Riggs' information went straight up to the Detroit PD and the state investigation. It was instrumental to a few of their arrests." He shrugged. "A Riggs, right? No one would have guessed. No one *did* guess."

I could feel my stomach turning itself in knots. I'd raked Jace over the coals, trying to get him to tell me why he'd stolen cars. I'd given him the bullshit about how he didn't fit the profile. And he hadn't said a word. "Someone should have told me," I said.

"It should have been in the file, I agree," John said. He looked at my face, which was probably red. "What's wrong?"

I shook my head. "It's just that I would have handled his

counseling differently. I, um, spent time talking with him about why he picked a life of crime."

"Ah," John said. "Well, I saw your report in my inbox, so no harm done, right?"

"Can I ask you something?"

He was heading for the door. "Sure, I guess."

"Why doesn't a CI get counseling like every other ex-con?"

John sighed. "I don't make the rules, Tara. I guess it's assumed that CI's aren't real criminals, in the standard sense, so their treatment is different."

"Jace Riggs might not be a real criminal, but he spent twenty months in prison," I argued. "He has to readjust exactly like every other con. He needs help just like anyone else. More, maybe. I mean, why did the system let him do time in the first place, when he was helping them get so many arrests?"

John was watching me talk, frowning. When he spoke, it was in the calm I'm-an-expert voice he no doubt used on his clients. "You seem rather upset about this."

"Do I?" I shook my head. "Pardon me if it seems unfair that the system would use Jace Riggs to get arrests, then hang him out to dry when he got caught. Then try to deny him help after he did his time. Pardon me if I point out that Jace Riggs got a raw deal."

"Tara," John said calmly, definitely in counselor mode now, "Jace Riggs really did steal those cars. He's a grown man who did illegal things and pleaded guilty to them in court. Maybe he would have had a tougher sentence if he *wasn't* a CI. Have you thought of that?"

I stared at him, knowing I looked like a fool, unable to stop my hot cheeks or my passionate words. "Someone should have *told* me," I insisted. Maybe it was the crazy day, but I couldn't stop myself. "If I'd known, maybe I could have actually helped him instead of filling out a bullshit form. I got into this job to *help* people. That's why I do it in the first place."

"He'll be fine." Now John's voice was firm. He hated emotion, and he certainly hated it when it was holding him up from going home for the day. "Jace Riggs is going to be just fine, whether he gets counseling or not. You can't help every single one of them, Tara. It's one of the facts of the job. The sooner you learn it, the longer you'll last in this career. Am I making myself clear?"

I choked my words down, felt them in the back of my throat as I swallowed them. "Yes. You're clear."

"Good. Now go home and have a glass of wine, and start over tomorrow." He turned and was gone, off to his family.

I did go home. And I intended to do as John said—have a glass of wine, maybe a bath, a nice dinner, watch some TV. My usual single girl's night in.

Instead, I let myself into my lonely little apartment, changed into casual jeans, a T-shirt, a sweater, and flip-flops, washed my face, brushed out my hair, and walked back out again. I got back in my car and drove across Westlake, across the train tracks that bisected the town, and I headed for Welmer Road. The big, ramshackle house where the Riggs family lived.

I wasn't Jace Riggs' counselor anymore.

Maybe now, we could finally have a conversation.

EIGHT

Tara

THE HOUSE WAS in bad shape, but I could see that someone was at least trying to improve it. The grass was mowed, and a large section had been pulled out and replanted with grass seed in an effort to kill all the weeds. There were a few new paving stones in the front walk and a stack of tools sat on the sagging front porch, like someone was planning to do work with them as soon as he was free.

I circled around the house to the back. Jace had said he lived in the guest house on the family property, and sure enough, behind the main house was a smaller building, big enough for just a few rooms. The day was receding into dusk, and the air smelled sweet. A few yards over, a dog barked. A quiet day in the neighborhood on the wrong side of the tracks.

I could see no light on in the guest house, no car parked in the cleared gravel space at the side of the house. I knocked on the door anyway and waited patiently. Funny that the idea of digging into Jace's file and finding his phone number felt like a breach of privacy to me—which was why I hadn't done it—yet this didn't. I was probably crazy and he would kick me off the property. I should probably go home.

Especially since, as it seemed, he wasn't even home. I left the guest house and walked back around the house, but instead of heading back to my car I mounted the steps to the sagging front porch and rang the bell for the main house.

Because apparently, when it came to Jace Riggs, I had no idea where to draw the line.

There were footsteps behind the door, and it was opened by a wildly good-looking man wearing a white tee and a low-slung pair of jeans. He had dark hair and high cheekbones and a bad-boy curl to his lip that probably slayed women for miles. I knew instantly that he was Jace's brother Luke, who Jace had said lived in the main house with his girlfriend. The two men didn't look exactly the same—Luke had a casual, lazy air, where Jace was all coiled-up tension—but the Riggs genes were there: size, muscles, smoldering good looks. The Riggs parents might be useless, if not abusive, but they produced downright gorgeous sons.

"Yeah?" Luke Riggs said, looking me up and down, in a way that was curious rather than sexual.

"Hi," I said, trying to sound like a halfway normal person. "I'm looking for Jace Riggs. Is he here?"

Luke blinked, and his curious gaze intensified. "You're looking for Jace?"

"I am," I said. "You're Luke, right?"

Now he was *very* curious, though he masked it with his lazy drawl. "You know who I am," he said slowly, "but I don't know who you are."

"Tara Montgomery," I said. I thought about sticking out my hand, then decided it would look too dorky with a guy this cool.

"I'm, um, an acquaintance of Jace's. I really need to talk to him. Is he here?"

Luke just stood there looking at me for a moment. I couldn't quite read his expression. "He's not here," he said finally. "He went out."

I blew out a breath. Damn it. "Where do you think I could find him?"

"No offense," Luke said, "but I don't know you, so I don't think I'm going to say."

It was then I realized what his expression was: distrust. "I'm not going to hurt him," I said. "I just want to talk."

Luke leaned a shoulder on the doorframe, still looking at me with that dark, distrustful gaze that had an edge of hostility to it. "I'm trying to figure out who you are," he said. "You're definitely someone official, because Jace doesn't have a girlfriend and women don't come around looking for him. You're not his PO. I'm tossed up between a cop or a social worker, and Jace doesn't need to talk to either one."

I opened my mouth to say something, I had no idea what, but a voice called from behind Luke's shoulder. "Luke? Who is it?"

A woman appeared in the doorway. She was blonde and gorgeous, even wearing yoga pants and an oversized T-shirt. She stepped next to Luke and looked at me curiously.

"A woman," Luke said, "looking for Jace."

The blonde's eyes went wide.

"She says her name is Tara Montgomery," Luke said. "You know a Tara Montgomery, Emily?"

The woman—Emily—looked thoughtful. "Doesn't ring a bell," she said to Luke. She turned to me. "Did you go to Westlake High?"

"Um, no," I said. "I went to private school."

Emily's eyes went wide again, and Luke elbowed her gently. "Cop or social worker," he said to her. "That's my guess."

"Look," I said, feeling my chances slipping away, "can you tell me where Jace is? I'm not a cop or a social worker. I really need to speak with him."

Emily glanced at Luke, took in the set of his jaw, then looked back at me. "Honey," she said, "come clean."

What was the deal with these two? "I'm his friend," I said.

"Jace doesn't have friends," Emily said bluntly. "He especially doesn't have good-looking, private school, *female* friends. So just say what you want, or Luke will send you on your way, and I don't blame him. Jace has already been to hell and back, and he doesn't need any more trouble."

So that was it. I saw it now: they were protective. Jace thought no one in his family gave a shit about him, but apparently someone did. I took a breath and rolled the dice. "Here's the deal," I said. "I was assigned by the court as his counselor, but when he came to see me I fucked it up. I really did. And I submitted my report and said nice things and I'm not his counselor anymore, but that isn't enough. I want to make it right. I need to apologize to him. That's all—just apologize." I looked back and forth between them. "Please."

The corner of Emily's pretty mouth twitched. She leaned against Luke, curling one arm casually over his shoulder, her hip against his. "I vote you tell her," she said to him.

I tried not to stare at the easy way she touched him, the way her body fit against his, the way he looked so relaxed with her leaning on him like that, like she was meant to be there. These two weren't just dating—they were in love.

And they were having sex, a lot of it. It was pretty much there for anyone to see. It made my throat close because even when I was engaged, I'd never had a relationship like that. I'd never leaned on Kyle without thinking the way Emily was leaning on Luke right now. I'd never felt so physically close to a man—even a man I was sleeping with—that I'd notched my hip against his.

Like we just totally belonged to each other. What must that feel like?

Emily obviously won Luke over by touching him—something I gathered wasn't new—because Luke said, "Okay, fine. He went to play pool at the Guardhouse. Left about two hours ago."

I knew the Guardhouse, a pool hall on the downtown Westlake strip. "Thank you," I said, turning to leave.

"Apologize," Luke said, and though his voice was even, I knew he meant it. "If you fucked up, tell him you're sorry. Emily is right. Jace is the last person who needs anyone's shit."

I nodded and turned away, heading for my car. I felt like I'd been put to the test, but I couldn't feel bad about it. In fact, it made me almost feel hopeful. Because someone really did care about Jace.

If only he could be made to believe it.

NINE

Jace

YOU'D THINK the Riggs men would be big drinkers, considering our upbringing. Our mothers bailed early—Ryan had a different mother than Dex, Luke, and me—and left us alone to grow up however we could. Predictably, we ran wild. We didn't follow very many rules growing up, but we ended up with surprisingly few vices. Sure, Dex knew a weed dealer on every block and had the alcohol tolerance of a solid slab of iron—he could do shots one by one until his eyes got a little unfocused, and then he'd fall into a peaceful sleep. But Ryan was an athlete, and now he was raising a seven-year-old son, so he didn't drink, and Luke only had the occasional beer.

As for me, my endlessly ticking brain never let me get truly fucked up. *Why are you doing this? Is this the right thing? Is it making you happy?* By the time I'd talked myself into getting hammered, I'd usually exhausted myself.

Tonight, I wanted to get wrecked.

Sitting and staring at nothing on a barstool sounded boring, so I took my beer to the pool room in the back of the Guardhouse and challenged all comers. I learned pool at thirteen, and I was fucking good at it. The lines and angles all made sense in my head. A pool shark once told me that to be good at pool was the sign of a wasted youth, and he was right. I'd gone to school, and I found it easy, but teachers hated me. After the fourth or fifth time a teacher assumed I was cheating when I got good marks, I gave up trying. I went to school occasionally, and the rest of the time I read books or played pool.

I am trying to figure out why a man who is intelligent and sensitive and kind would steal cars and fuck up his life.

A guy I vaguely recognized from high school challenged me with thirty bucks on the line; I beat him easily. Then I beat him two out of three. Next up was John Bowmer, well-known Westlake dart champion and barfly. At thirty, John's teeth were cigarette yellow and he'd had at least one divorce. His pool skills were not equal to his dart skills, so I beat him for twenty bucks and sent him back to the bar.

I was now eighty bucks richer and on my third beer. I was prickly and pissed off after that session with Tara Montgomery. I was mad at myself and at her, but mostly at me. Her words hovered in my brain, cutting like razor blades. *I am trying to figure out why a man who is intelligent and sensitive and kind would steal cars and fuck up his life. I feel sorry for whoever gets you next.* I took another deep swallow of beer.

The Guardhouse was popular, and it was busy, so I got more contestants. There were even women here, a few of them eyeing me. Fuck. Twenty months in jail. If I could get out of my own head long enough, maybe it was time.

I feel sorry for whoever gets you next.

"Riggs." I knew that voice. I turned to see Derek Payton, who had been in the same grade as me in high school. We Riggs boys were from the wrong side of the tracks in Westlake—literally, Westlake had railroad tracks with a wrong side and a right side—so we were out of place at Westlake High. Derek had looked down his nose at me, just like everyone else. What made it extra annoying was that I happened to know Derek had a side business selling meth, so he wasn't really any better than me. I knew too many people's dirty secrets in this fucking town.

Still, it would be satisfying to beat Derek, so I said, "Derek. You up for a challenge?"

Derek's gaze flicked down to my cue, then back up. "Shooting pool, huh? I see you've been real productive since you got out. Sounds like something your brother Dex would do."

"Dex sucks at pool." Dex was good, actually, but I was better.

Derek gave me a smile that had no humor in it, and I remembered the time we'd gotten into a fistfight in tenth grade. I won. Maybe he hadn't gotten over it. "You're the brother that ended up in jail," he said. "Funny."

"Not really," I said.

"Lots of time to read your weird-ass books in there, I guess," Derek said. "Just don't bend over to get the soap, right?"

Anger flared up my throat, and I wanted to break my pool cue over his head. Not because anything had happened to me in prison—it hadn't—but because he was so fucking smug. The thing about hitting rock bottom, I'd learned, is that it can happen to anyone. Fucking *anyone*. It didn't matter who you were, or how good you were, or what side of the tracks you came from, or how superior you were. Anyone could end up where I was right now.

Then again, I'd made some choices, hadn't I?

I opened my mouth, probably to say something stupid, and then I stopped. Because behind Derek's shoulder, the door to the bar opened and Tara Montgomery walked in.

She had changed out of her work clothes. She wore jeans on

her slim legs and a white T-shirt under a light summer cardigan of navy blue. Her long brown hair was down, soft over her shoulders and down her back. Flip-flops were on her feet, and I could see her bare toes beneath the hem of her jeans. Her toenails were painted dark purple.

Every guy in the bar noticed her one by one as she spotted me and crossed the room. I couldn't do anything but stare—I was too shocked at the sight of her. Why was she here? At the Guardhouse? Looking for me?

Derek noticed her at the last minute. He turned around and his eyebrows went up. Tara barely spared him a glance.

"Jace," she said to me in her blunt way, "can we talk?"

She didn't even have makeup on, and she was fucking beautiful. Derek noticed. "Hi there," he said, butting in. "You Jace's girlfriend? You don't seem like his type."

Tara turned to him, unimpressed. "What type is that?" She shook her head. "You know what? Don't answer." She turned back to me. "Well?"

I felt myself smiling. She'd actually come looking for me; she must have. Even if she'd come to chew me out, I was still happy to see her. "You want to play pool?" I asked her.

She looked me up and down—all the way up and down, and I realized we weren't in session anymore. "No," she said. "I want to get out of here. Is your tab paid up?"

"Yes," I said.

She took the pool cue from my hand and put it back on the rack. "Honey, let's go."

What the hell could I do? I was three beers in, and she had those jeans on, and she'd said *Honey, let's go*. I followed her through the bar and out the door.

"Impressive," I said to her when we got outside and stood on the street, "but you shouldn't go into places like that. All of those guys were staring at you."

"Maybe I like pool," Tara said.

I slid my hands into my back pockets and looked at her. "You hate pool," I said, taking a guess.

Her lips pressed into a line, and I knew I was right. I smiled again, and she looked at me closely. "Are you drunk?" she asked.

"Three beers," I confessed. "I feel pretty good, and I won a hundred and twenty bucks. Are you going to tell my PO?"

She shook her head. "I'm not your counselor anymore, Jace."

"What does that mean? I thought I was going to have to go to sessions until I'm ninety."

"Yeah, that." She bit her lip. "I feel bad about that. Where can we talk?"

My place was out of the question, and so was hers, wherever it was. We were too combustible right now; the air practically smelled like sulfur. "Let's take a walk," I said.

We walked down the sidewalk toward the park. It was dark out, getting late, the air warm as a breath, the wind hushing in the trees. The peak heat of summer was gone, and now we had the sweet-smelling bittersweet feel of September coming. In my bedroom, in the guest house, I kept my windows open every night because part of me couldn't stand being parted from the fresh air.

The park was dark and quiet, private. We took the main path toward the center, and then Tara dropped onto a park bench. I sat beside her, sprawling my legs out, and waited for her to say what she had come to say.

"Okay." She squared her shoulders. "First, I wrote the report on you and sent it to the judge. I gave you a clean bill of mental health. I told him you are adjusting just fine."

I tilted my head and looked at her. "What? Why did you do that?"

She didn't look at me; she looked straight ahead, so I was free to stare at her perfect profile in the dim light. "Well, you *are* in good mental health," she said logically. "Also, I was a jerk in session and I owed you that."

"No," I said. "You were a jerk because I was a jerk first. I call dibs."

"Jace," she said. She sighed, shook her head, and glanced at me. "You deserved better."

That was when I figured it out. Why she'd sought me out, why she'd come to the Guardhouse, why we were sitting in the park right now. Why she was saying sorry. It wasn't because of me. It never had been.

"Shit," I said to her. "They told you."

TEN

Tara

HE SOUNDED SURPRISED AND ANNOYED, and there was something else in the undertone of his voice. I thought maybe it was hurt, but it was so fleeting and hard to read that I couldn't be sure.

I looked into his eyes. I'd been avoiding them, because it was always Jace's eyes that stripped me of my defenses. But I held his gaze and said, "They told me. They should have told me before our first session. It would have been different if they had. I would have—"

"Stop." His voice was flat. "They aren't supposed to tell you. That's what the word *confidential* means in *confidential informant*. The more people who know, the more chances I have to get killed for it."

"Your file is confidential," I said. "Believe me."

Jace looked at me coolly and steadily. The happy, unfocused, slightly drunk look was gone; he was dead sober now. "I wondered why I got put in the counseling program," he said. "It wasn't supposed to happen. They keep us out because the fewer people who know who we are, the better. I thought I was a special case." A swift shot of pain crossed his eyes, then was gone again. "How did you track me down, by the way? It must have been Luke."

"It was," I said. "I told him I wanted to find you. To apologize."

He seemed to calculate something. "Luke doesn't know," he said. "None of my brothers do."

I nodded. "How did it start?" I asked. "The informing? Since I already know about it, you can tell me."

He looked away and quickly drummed his fingers on his jean-clad knee. Always thinking, thinking. This man looked like an everyday bad boy, but he was so damned complicated, I didn't think I'd ever peel away all of his layers. "I guess you know my mother left," he said. "That must be in the file."

"Briefly, yes."

"Well, *briefly* describes how long she was in my life. Dad raised us. Which meant basically we were on our own."

I tried to imagine that and couldn't. I wasn't close to my parents, but at least I'd had them.

Jace went on. "When I was seven, I made a big mistake. I asked Dad if I could get a bike. All the other kids had one, and I wanted one." He drummed his fingers on his knee again, then stopped. "Dad laughed in my face and said that was a pussy thing to ask for. You have to understand that *pussy* is Dad's biggest insult, next to *faggot*. My father is all class."

I looked down at my lap. No, I couldn't imagine it.

"Dex was there," Jace said. "He was nine. He defended me, which wasn't his usual M.O. He told Dad that a bike wasn't a pussy thing, it was badass. And that at least I'd be able to pedal away from him faster." He lifted his hand and traced the shell of his ear. "Dad punched him hard, right here. Right on the ear. Dex fell over—it was the surprise, I think, because Dex was a tough kid. Of the four of us, he took the most hits. He didn't say anything and he didn't cry, but his ear was bright red for the rest of the day. My big brother had stood up for me for once in his life, and Dad knocked him down for it."

My heart was breaking. "Jace."

He shrugged, his shoulders graceful under his leather jacket. "The next day I went to Riggs Auto and I opened the till and took the money to buy a bike. And I didn't feel bad about it." I raised my gaze and found him looking at me. He continued. "After high school, Dad gave me a job at Riggs Auto. When he got involved with the stolen car shit, he told me to shut up and do as I was told or I'd be in big trouble. So I shut up and did as I was told, and then I went to the cops and offered to tell them anything they wanted to know. And I didn't feel bad about that either."

I shook my head. "What about the stealing? How did that start?"

"Dad told me to do it," Jace said. "By then I was overhearing important shit. Everyone saw me as the quiet Riggs brother, the obedient one, so they said whatever around me. I was getting information on drug shipments, warehouses, illegal firearms deals. If I said no, I was out of the circle. So I stole cars." He ran a hand through his hair, and I caught a glimpse of his silver rings in the moonlight. "I actually was good at it. That part was true. Yeah, it was illegal. But I made some good money and I never hurt anyone. It was fun to be really good at something for once."

"They let you go to prison," I said, "after you gave them all that information."

He looked at me thoughtfully, tilting his head. "If you steal cars, you might spend some time sitting in a cell. That's how the world works."

"Well, it sucks," I said, forcefully.

He smiled at me, and it was a little sad, and I wanted to climb into his lap and put my mouth on his until he stopped looking sad and instead looked like he wanted to fuck me right here on this bench. I wondered if I'd ever make him look like that. I wondered if some other woman made him look like that, and who she was, and whether she was beautiful.

I don't fuck, Jace had said. He'd never explained why.

As if he was reading my mind, he leaned in toward me, his breath against the shell of my ear. He smelled like leather and beer and hot, sexy man. "You can't help me, Tara," he said. "You think you can, but you can't."

I swallowed hard. "It's my job."

"Not anymore it isn't." He inhaled softly, and I knew he was scenting me like I'd scented him. He changed position and his lips ghosted over mine, the touch so light I almost thought I'd imagined it. I inhaled in surprise, but he pulled back, still looking in my eyes. "My broken parts will stay broken," he said. "You can't do anything about that."

"Because that's the way the world works?" I asked.

"Pretty much."

I gave it back to him. I leaned and brushed my lips over his, petal-light.

"Watch me," I said.

ELEVEN

Jace

THE THUNDERBIRD, I decided, was an awesome fucking car. It needed work on just about everything, because it had obviously been sitting parked and rusting somewhere for years, but it wasn't anything I couldn't handle. In between working on cars for actual paying customers at Riggs Auto, I'd sneak over to it and spend half an hour here, an hour there, tweaking and caressing it. It was ugly and it wasn't classic, but the metal trim and that fucking V6 were sexy as hell. It was growing on me. I'd never had a car that was my baby before, but this one sure was.

I was under the hood working the engine when Luke came over. "You got a delivery," he said.

I pulled my head out from under the hood and frowned at him. "What?"

"Delivery," Luke said again. He was wiping his hands with a rag, his coveralls off and stowed in a locker. We were almost done for the day. "Up front. You have to sign for it. They won't let me do it."

There was nothing I could think of that it could be, but I wiped my hands on my coveralls and unzipped them—it was freaking hot back here, airless in the day's heat. I was wearing a T-shirt that showed my tatted arms, and I let the coverall drop to my waist as I walked to the front of the shop. There was a courier there, a young redheaded woman with an envelope in her hand. "Are you John Riggs?" she asked when she saw me.

I tried not to wince. The only time I heard my given name was at the doctor's office or in court. Even my parole officer called me Jace. "Yeah, that's me."

"Sign, please." She handed me the envelope and a pen. I signed the slip, and when I handed it back to her, I saw that her cheeks were pink. "Thanks," she said. "Have a nice day."

I frowned as she walked out the door, but Luke, who was standing in the doorway, only laughed softly. "She was totally into you, man."

"She doesn't know me," I pointed out.

"That's not how it works," Luke said. "You see someone *before* you know them. See?"

"Thank you, O Wise One," I said, turning the envelope over in my hands. It was stamped from the Michigan Correctional System. Yeah, this was going to be fun, whatever it was.

"If you paid attention, you'd get laid more often," Luke pointed out, ignoring the envelope I was holding. "Women dig you, Jace. You have that soulful poet thing going on."

"I look like a con," I said absently, staring at the envelope. I'd already signed for it. Did I even want to open this thing?

"Sure, don't take my advice," Luke said. "There are women everywhere, you know. Single women. Good-looking women. If you just got your nose out of a book or from under the hood of a car, you'd clean up."

I looked at him, finally distracted from the fresh hell that was probably this envelope. "Maybe I already clean up," I said. It's a reflex when you have three brothers. You can't show weakness.

"You live in the guest house out my window," Luke said. "You don't clean up. I would know."

For some reason, the first thought that came to my mind was Tara Montgomery. The way she'd brushed her mouth over mine. *Watch me.* I tried to remember the last time a woman had put her mouth on mine, and it was so far back it was too depressing to contemplate.

"What's it to you?" I asked Luke. *Deflecting,* Tara would have called it. "Why do you care how often I get laid?"

Luke shrugged. "I'm just trying to help you out."

"Dude, you were hung up on Emily Parker for *eight years.* You're hardly an expert in playing the field."

Score one for me. Luke hadn't been celibate for those eight years—he'd never discussed it, but I'd bet my sweet Thunderbird on it—but he wasn't about to dispute the fact that he'd been hung up on the one and only love of his life. "Okay," Luke said, "if you don't trust my advice, you should ask Ryan. You know he's banged most of the female population of Westlake between the ages of twenty-five and thirty."

True. Ryan *had* cleaned up during his high school years, in a big way. But then he'd gotten a girl pregnant and had a kid at twenty, and four years later she'd dumped their son on his doorstep to raise, so all of that had put the brakes on Ryan's big-league sex life. "At least he knows more about women than you do," I said to Luke. "Or maybe I should ask Dex."

We both laughed at that. Dex was crazy—do-not-pass-Go, flat-out fucking crazy. Every woman who had the balls to go near Dex had been crazy too. The few brief dating relationships he'd had had ended up in screaming fights and tears, thousands of phone calls on repeat and threats to call the cops. Something about Dex made women absolutely lose their shit, and not in a good way. Maybe it was something he put in their water.

"Okay, do *not* ask Dex for dating advice," Luke said. "But go after that courier and ask her out. I'm telling you, she'll say yes."

"Or here's another idea," I said. "I'll do whatever the fuck I want, just like I always do." But damn, he was right. I was starting to see that. I was twenty-five, for God's sake. I was out of prison, and I wasn't dead. I'd started to think it, but now I was getting more convinced. It was time.

Tara Montgomery made me think it was time.

Except I wasn't going to have Tara Montgomery. Not now, not ever.

She saw me as a project. Even though she wasn't my counselor anymore, she saw me as someone to fix, someone to save. And it wasn't going to work. I knew that already—because I wasn't fixable.

"What's in the envelope?" Luke asked, breaking me out of my thoughts.

Shit. The envelope. I ripped it open and pulled out the letter inside.

It stated that the Michigan Correctional System had ruled that my parole obligations had been discharged in full. I no longer had to report to my parole officer. I no longer had to follow the stringent rules and report in. I was finished with the correctional system entirely. I was a free man.

My hands went numb. My vision blurred for a second, and I couldn't breathe. Then I forced in a breath and blinked.

I owed you that, Tara had said. I wasn't stupid. I knew full well that I was getting this letter because of the report she'd written about me and sent up the line. The report she'd written after the *second* time we'd had an argument in session. If she hadn't written that report, and sent it so quickly, I would still be stuck in the gears of the system, waiting for something to happen.

She was trying to fix me—but for a second all I could see was Tara. The way her dark hair fell over her shoulders, her slim body, the line of her lower lip, the way her eyes flashed when she was mad, the way she looked at me sometimes in a way I couldn't fathom. The way she smelled of pure, sweet female skin.

We were done. I'd already known that, but this paper made it official. We were over.

But because of this paper, we were not fucking over.

At the very least, she deserved a thank you.

Maybe I needed to give her one.

TWELVE

Tara

IT WAS FRIDAY, and for the first time in a long time, I was looking forward to the weekend. As I finished my last appointment and started clearing off my desk and wrapping up the last few emails, I realized that I'd been letting work take over my life. I usually stayed late on Fridays, working ahead on my own time, and I often took work home—case files, session plans, research and articles to read. I'd spend my weekend ensconced in my little apartment, working and doing housework until Monday came again.

It had been like that since the breakup with Kyle, the cancellation of the wedding plans. That made some sense, even though the breakup had been my idea. But when I thought back, I realized the pattern went back much farther. Those last months with Kyle, I'd withdrawn into work, made it the center of my life, probably to avoid facing the problems in our relationship head-on. I hadn't been happy, and instead of taking it out on Kyle and having fights, I'd simply gone to work.

I didn't know what had changed, but tonight I wanted *out* of here. Summer was ending. Maybe I'd take a walk. Maybe I'd read a book—a novel, not an academic book. Maybe I'd make popcorn and watch mindless TV and do my nails. I was nearly jumpy, my blood singing, my skin tingling, all at the thought of two whole days to myself.

Okay, fine, maybe I *did* know what had changed. Jace Riggs had kissed me, sort of. I'd sort of kissed him back. It was nothing, but I still felt like I was on a rollercoaster, climbing to the top of the peak and about to go over. He was an ex-con car thief who smelled like leather and bonfire smoke, and when he'd leaned in close to me, when I'd felt that light brush of his lips and his beard, I'd been giddier than I'd ever been in two years with Kyle.

All of it was stupid, and all of it was in my head, but it had happened, and it still put me in a good mood. So, of course, my mother chose that moment to call me.

"Mom," I said, picking up the phone because if I didn't, she'd simply call again. "What's up? I'm just heading home from work."

"Tara," my mother said. "Your father and I would like you to come out to dinner."

My spine tightened, like it always did when my mother issued an order. There was never a *hi honey, how are you* from my mother—she always told me immediately what she wanted me to do, and there was always something. My father simply never called at all.

"What's the occasion?" I asked Mom, trying to stay polite.

"The occasion is that we haven't seen you in two months," Mom said. "We'd like to see you and get an update on your progress."

Honestly, this was how my mother talked. *An update on your progress.* My parents weren't bad people, but two people who should never have been parents in the first place. It was so patently obvious they were unsuited to parenthood that I'd figured it out by the time I was fourteen. "I'm doing fine," I said to Mom. I was pulling my purse from my drawer and toeing off the heels I'd worn, replacing them with the flats I'd brought in my bag.

"Regardless," Mom said, "we should have dinner at Aldi's."

Aldi's was one of Westlake's most expensive restaurants. My parents were both investment brokers, and money had always been plentiful—we weren't filthy rich, but I'd had more money than, say, Jace Riggs. Enough to go to private school and get a college degree, though both of my parents completely disapproved of my career choice. They'd been hoping their only child would be a surgeon. Counseling the downtrodden, the mentally ill, the ex-cons, and people who were on the skids of life was *not* what they'd imagined for my future.

I'd grown further apart from my parents since I started this career; they didn't want to talk about it, which meant I couldn't talk to them about the biggest thing in my everyday life. The breakup with Kyle hadn't helped at all—they'd at least wanted to see me "settled" with someone unobjectionable like Kyle, and when I'd called the whole thing off, they'd been painfully confused. They still didn't get it.

So I knew what this dinner would be. They'd ask for an update on my life; I'd tell them I was still single and still a counselor, and the rest of the night would be bitter tension. There were no two people more rigid, more unforgiving, than my parents.

I left my office and locked it, the phone crooked between my shoulder and my ear. "Maybe we can do it some other time, Mom," I said, feeling my happy Friday night slip through my fingers.

"Tonight is the only night your father can make it," my mother declared. "He has golf Saturday and Sunday."

"Dad doesn't care about dinner," I said. I meant to toss the words off, but they were true. I could see my father once a year at Christmas and he'd be fine with it. I'd dropped off his radar when I got my counseling degree. I took the stairwell two flights down to the street because the elevator was known to cut off phone signals.

"Tara, it's been two months," Mom repeated.

"Is there a schedule?" I said.

"Laura Ferrano's daughter visits her every Saturday," Mom replied.

I felt my jaw go tight. How many times had we had this argument? Too many times to count. My mother's requests—her commands—were always based on the idea of what behavior was correct rather than a true desire to see me. The older I got, the more correctness was required, based on where she thought I was supposed to be in life, and no matter how much I argued or how I worded it, I couldn't get her to see it. The minute the topic opened, her defenses would go up. I loved my mother—I loved both my parents—but she was exhausting.

I exited the stairwell door to the street. "Mom—" I stopped.

Jace Riggs was sitting on the bench on the other side of the sidewalk. He was sitting with his elbows on his jean-clad knees, his hands dangling between his legs. He was wearing a T-shirt with a soft, slim-cut black hoodie over it that skimmed every muscled line of his torso and arms. His hair was clean and combed, his beard trimmed close to his jaw, and his gray gaze had lit on me.

I froze with the phone at my ear and held his gaze. There was no way it was a mistake; Jace was here for me. Waiting.

"Tara?" Mom said.

"I can't come to dinner, Mom," I said. "I have plans."

"Plans?" Mom said in disbelief. "With who?"

No, oh no. I wasn't telling my mother about Jace Riggs. "A friend," I told her.

"What friend?"

"I have to go. He's here."

"He?"

I hung up and walked toward him. "Jace," I said.

He watched me come forward. When I got close he lifted his elbows from his knees and leaned back on the bench, stretching one arm casually over the back—a pose that did beautiful things to his shoulder muscles. "Are you finished with work?" he asked.

"I am," I said. "You could have called, you know."

It almost sounded like a criticism, and I didn't mean it to. The butterflies had started in my stomach and I was freaking giddy again.

"I didn't want to interrupt you while you were working," Jace said. His deep, almost sad gaze flicked past my shoulder and back to my face again. "Besides, I only have the reception number."

Right. He hadn't wanted to call and talk to reception because I wasn't his counselor anymore. This wasn't business—it was personal. I felt the giddiness warm up into a slow, pleasurable pulse between my legs. "True," I said to him. "I'll give you my number."

Our gazes locked. Jesus. I could talk to a dozen people a day and say a hundred different things and not remember any of it. Yet every word I spoke with Jace Riggs was laced with meaning. I'd offered him my number, but I'd also offered him my trust and my privacy, and he knew it. For a woman who dealt with men on the edge almost every day, my privacy was my most prized possession; there were too many stories about counselors like me being stalked, threatened.

Jace's gaze dropped to where I'd dropped my phone in my purse. "Are you busy?" he asked.

He meant, *Was that a man you were talking to?* Seriously. "That was my mother," I said. "She asked me to dinner, and I said I had plans."

Wariness now, just a flicker of it, but it was a common Jace expression. "Do you?"

"I have plans with you," I said.

He rubbed his fingertips over his chin, rasping them over his beard, his rings gleaming in the sunlight. I'd seen Jace under my office fluorescents, and I'd seen him at night, but I'd never seen him in the sun. He was just as beautiful under any light. "Tara," he said, my name vibrating through me as it came from him. "Tell me the truth. Am I bothering you?"

This man. This fucking man. "No," I told him, my voice raw. "You aren't bothering me. Are you hungry? Let's get dinner."

THIRTEEN

Tara

WE DIDN'T GO to Aldi's, or anywhere expensive. We didn't even go somewhere romantic. We went to a tiny Greek place five blocks from my office, where the tables were small and jammed together, the food was homemade and cheap, and you could get a bottle of good wine for less than ten dollars. We ordered the wine and split the bottle. "You said you don't drink," I said as he poured us each a glass.

"I didn't mean never," Jace said. "I just meant not all the time. Tonight I'm driving, though. Luke lent me his car."

"You don't have one?"

"Weird for a car thief, right?" It was said with an edge of humor, and he quirked an eyebrow at me. "I sold it to pay my lawyer's bills before I went in. Now I'm out and I have to get one the old-fashioned, legal way. Luke got a secondhand one through the garage, but it isn't road-ready yet. I'm working on it."

This, I could tell, was a subject near and dear to him. His expression almost got soft, like he was talking about a girl he liked. "You love cars," I observed.

"Cars are my blood," Jace said, "but we already talked about me. I told you, I'm fucking boring."

I laughed. "Jace, you've had a crazy life. You're not exactly boring."

He put the wine bottle down. "I got papers in the mail. They said that I'm not on parole anymore." His gray eyes caught mine and held them. "That's you," he said softly. "Don't think I don't know it."

I felt myself flush. "You deserve it."

"Still, thank you." He leaned back in his chair. "So you're not behind the desk anymore. You get to sit in the hot seat. We already picked me apart. Now you get to talk."

I sipped my wine. "All right. It's strangely hard to begin, though. I'm never the one doing the talking."

Jace just waited, the way I always did in a session, and I took another sip of wine. I'd said it lightly, but I realized it was true—I wasn't used to anyone expecting me to talk. Kyle was long gone, and as our relationship deteriorated we'd done very little talking. Time with my parents was usually spent with me silent while they talked, which was why I dreaded it. I had work colleagues, old college acquaintances, and almost no friends.

And, now, Jace. Whatever he was.

He'd already seen the worst of me within the first hour of meeting me, so I found myself relaxing. Jace was the last person to judge. I took one more sip of wine for fortification and started to talk.

I told him about my upbringing, about my parents. About how I'd had a good childhood, safe and free from want, but how from an early age my parents had driven me to try and be something I wasn't. How they used their disapproval and disappointment to try and get me to change my course. How I loved my parents dearly—of course I did—but they drove me crazy every time I tried to talk to them.

Jace listened, interrupting with only one question. "They don't want you to be a counselor?"

"They hate it," I said. "They think I've wasted my potential. It doesn't matter how many times I explain that helping people who need it is not wasting my potential at all—it falls on deaf ears. I've given up trying."

Our meals had arrived, and he slowly stirred his spoon through his soup, which was the only thing he had ordered. "I don't know much about having parents," he said, "but you're the only one who can live your life."

Of course he didn't know much about having parents. His mother had left and his father was in prison. "I'm lucky to have them at all," I said.

"Maybe, but being lucky to have them and living your life for them are two different things."

"Is that what you think, counselor?" I said. My tone was light, teasing. I couldn't help it—I was flirting with him.

Jace stopped stirring and looked up at me, taking in my tone, and then he smiled a little. A spark of hot mischief lit his gaze, and I felt it all the way from the back of my neck down my spine, between my legs and down them.

"That's what I think," he said, his voice a little rough.

I gulped my wine again. It was going to my head, but in the best way: I felt relaxed, happy, immensely pleased by the gorgeous eye candy sitting across from me, the muscled line of his shoulders clear beneath the hoodie that fit him like a second skin. "Do you ever flirt?" I asked him. "Or do you just smolder?"

That spark of mischief again. "I guess I don't flirt," he said. "Apparently when I meet a sexy woman, I pick fights with her instead."

I waved a hand casually. "Bygones," I said, my voice coming out strangled because I was feeling every word he said all over my skin.

He laughed softly, and I felt *that* on my skin too. He'd called me sexy. I knew I wasn't awful, but I hadn't felt *sexy* in so, so long —Jesus, I couldn't even remember. I felt competent and professional and determined, but otherwise I felt numb. I had things to get done and work to do, all of which was fine, but it was like I'd vanished below the waist. Nothing existed down there—except, of course, for the occasional morning fantasy of the man across from me fucking me. And now I was remembering that again, and I had another rush of pleasure.

"Tell me about the asshole you almost married," Jace said, putting his spoon in his soup.

It was a splash of cold water, but even mention of Kyle couldn't quite kill my buzz. "Did I say he was an asshole?"

He gave me an innocent look. "You know, I don't really remember."

"I didn't. I said he was very nice, or something like that. And he was."

"Very nice?" Jace said, his voice low. "That's it?"

The wine was gone—it didn't escape me that I'd drunk most of the bottle—and I took a bite of my chicken, which was delicious. "I'm not sure what to tell you about Kyle."

"Tell me the truth."

There was raw power in those words; I'd used them on him in session. Why was that? Did we tell each other the truth so rarely in our daily lives? Was that what we had to do to get by?

"The truth is that I only sort of loved him," I told Jace. "He was a decent person. But that isn't enough for a marriage. I knew it in my gut the minute I said yes, and it only got worse as we started planning the wedding, planning where we would live, how many kids we would have. It was like you just said, the difference between appreciating someone and living your life for them. It wasn't good enough." I sighed and scrubbed a hand through my hair. "And there's guilt in that, because it makes me sound like I think I'm such hot shit. But I remind myself that if I spent our marriage miserable, I'd make him miserable too. So in a way I spared him. And it goes round and round and round."

Jace rubbed his fingers over his beard, listening.

"And the truth is," I added, "the sex was terrible."

Jace went still. His eyebrows rose. I had his full, undivided attention now.

"Terrible?" he said.

"Godawful," I replied, and it wasn't the wine that made me say it. It was the rush of truth. *Tell me something true,* Jace had asked of me in session. Well, he was going to get it. "It wasn't his fault, or anyone's, but it was terrible. We didn't fit. I never orgasmed. It was so bad that I thought for a long time that it was me, that I didn't like sex, period. That it just wasn't something I was interested in. And that wasn't fair to Kyle, so I got good at faking."

"Jesus," Jace said.

"And then one night he watched football until late, and then he crawled into bed with me, and I realized I didn't want to. I just didn't want to. Not with him. Because there's a big difference between liking and respecting someone and wanting them inside you. A very, very big fucking difference."

"I get that," Jace said.

I put my fork down and stared at him. "Do you?"

"Yeah, I do," he said. "You're supposed to see sex as not a big deal. Some guy puts his dick in you, so what? He's nice, he cares about you, he's trying to make you happy. Frankly, you're being too nice about him. He should never have fucked you if you didn't like it, if you had to fake it."

"I didn't tell him."

"If he loves you, he should know. He should be paying attention. That's his fucking job."

Jesus. I wasn't going to survive this night. I wasn't. "Kyle wasn't evil," I said, though I had no idea why I was defending him. It felt automatic. "He never understood why I was unhappy, why I left. I think he still doesn't understand it."

"Then he's stupid," Jace said simply. He tapped his temple. "Pick a guy with brains next time, Tara. Doctor, heal thyself."

I was melting like wax beneath the table. "Tell me something true, Jace," I said.

"Like what?"

"Tell me why you said you don't fuck."

He didn't even look surprised. He thought it over. "No, I won't tell you that," he said.

"Was it true?"

"Yeah," he said. "I don't. I'm pretty quiet, and I don't get a lot of opportunities. But the opportunities I get, I turn down."

Deep inside me, it was like someone had flipped a switch. I'd been turned on before, high on the crazy feeling of anticipation I had around him. Now I was hot as lava, a serious hotness that almost hurt. I wanted to pry Jace Riggs open and make him tell me everything. I wanted to be the one he didn't turn down. I wanted to be the one this complicated man couldn't resist. I thought I was almost there—but maybe, just maybe, not quite.

"Why?" I pressed him. "Why do you turn them down?" Not that I wanted him taking any woman up on an offer. Sitting here now, across from him, the visual made me angry and ill. "You were locked up so long, it can't be easy to say no."

He ran a hand through his hair, his long fingers sliding through the soft strands. "This again," he said. "Everyone thinks going to prison gives you a dick that won't stay down. Like it rampages out of control or something. My dick goes down when I tell it to. It goes up when I let it. It's called being a guy with a fucking brain. No one seems to get that."

"Who has an opinion about your dick?" I asked him, and now I was picturing it—and oh god, what a visual.

"Luke," Jace answered me, oblivious to the images of him naked that were going through my head. "Friends from before who try to throw women at me. Every guy who knows where I've been, basically. And now you."

"I don't," I argued. "I don't have an opinion about it."

Jace smiled at me, slow and easy.

"Okay," he said. "Finish your dinner."

FOURTEEN

Jace

WE WERE IN MY CAR—LUKE'S car, actually, a black Dodge Charger. I'd been at the restaurant with Tara, and we were talking. The conversation somehow became about my dick. We'd switched the subject again, talked about other things, but the topic of sex had hovered over us, smothering us like steam. I'd turned her on, something I hadn't started the evening intending to do but liked a whole hell of a fucking lot.

But I knew the situation. We weren't a thing. We could take this farther, push it to its limits, but anything we did would be one night. She was Tara, and I was me. We could fuck, maybe, but she'd be vaguely embarrassed afterward about being with a guy like me. We'd go our separate ways, and Tara would find some other guy to be with, and I'd go home to the guest house and overthink it.

And that was okay for her, maybe. A bad boy distraction for a night after her shitty breakup. But it wasn't enough for me.

With Tara, it would never be enough for me.

In the meantime, I liked talking to her. She was smart and self-deprecating and sometimes funny. She was vulnerable and raw, and she was tough and capable at the same time, a woman who didn't let me give her any shit. She could make an insightful comment you'd never thought of in one breath, and a dick joke in the next. She was fucking fascinating.

She'd drunk most of the wine at dinner, too much for her to drive home. So I had to drive her, leaving her car parked at her office for her to pick up the next day. Her eyes went wide at the sight of Luke's Charger because, honestly, the Charger is a woman magnet. Not that Luke was attracting any women anymore, except Emily.

Even though the car wasn't mine, it felt good to be driving. Ryan had taught me to drive at fourteen, the two of us spinning around the lot behind Riggs Auto. He'd been fifteen at the time. We Riggs brothers knew cars before we knew almost anything else.

After she gave me directions, Tara was quiet on the way to her place, though it wasn't an awkward quiet. She looked out the window, her shoulders relaxed against the back of the passenger seat, and she seemed to be thinking something through. I let her work through it.

She lived in an apartment in a low-rise building, a nice enough place for single professionals to live. The front lawn was nicely maintained and there were Corollas and Focuses in the parking lot. I'd just come from prison, then a halfway house in downtown Detroit for cons and addicts. If Tara lived here long enough, she'd probably meet a nice up-and-coming lawyer or a divorced accountant looking to settle down. I pulled into the driveway of Tara's building and tried not to think about it.

Tara was quiet for another long minute. She didn't get out of the car. "Jace," she said.

"Yeah," I said.

"I'm not going to invite you in, because I already know I'm one of the women you're going to turn down."

It was like a stab to the gut, those words. For a second it was so painful I almost closed my eyes. I could picture taking her inside, going to her apartment. Undressing her and laying her on her bed and having her until morning. It would be fire, and we would do fucking *everything*. And for a little while, she'd be mine.

For a little while.

"I'm not coming in," I told her.

She blew out a breath. "Okay then," she said. "I guess I'll do this here."

"Do what?"

She surprised me. She unbuckled her seatbelt and crawled over the gear shift, settling herself into my lap. Suddenly she was everywhere, the smell of her skin, the fall of her hair, her knees gripping my hips. My mind went mostly blank, but I had the presence of mind to push the seat back as far as it would go so she wouldn't bump her ass on the steering wheel.

She pressed into my lap and I almost sucked in a breath as my cock woke up all the way. I put my hands on her hips, whether to push her away or pull her closer I had no idea. She leaned forward and ran her fingertips over the beard on my jaw. I felt that touch in every nerve of my body.

"Tara," I said.

"Jesus, Jace," she said, and then she leaned down and kissed me.

It was fire. She cupped my jaw and our mouths opened, my tongue sweeping inside her as she sucked on me. Her long hair fell over us like a veil, and I could smell her clean shampoo. I slid my hand beneath her shirt and up her back, feeling the dip of her spine as she shivered and kissed me harder. Then I ran my hand back down, over the curve of her lower back, then down over her ass, which I gripped hard, pushing her hips into mine, letting her get the friction of my cock against her.

She gasped and moaned into my mouth. She squirmed and moved her hips, changing the angle, getting the pressure harder and more directly on her clit. I was hard as iron and I pressed her into me again, letting her practically feel the pulse of my blood through the clothes we were wearing. I moved my other hand under her shirt, brushing her waist, her belly, then up to one small breast, which I squeezed hard as she moaned into my mouth again. I brushed my thumb over her nipple through her bra and she made a helpless little sound, pressing her clit harder against me.

I moved my hand out from under her shirt. I kept my other hand on her ass, pressing her into me. I broke the kiss, gently cupped her face, and ran my thumb over her reddened lips, pushing it into the warm heat of her mouth. She sucked on it as I leaned in and kissed her neck, letting my beard scrape her soft skin, sucking her flesh into my mouth just enough to make her wince and squirm again.

She sucked on my thumb until I slid it out and put my mouth back over hers, replacing it with my tongue. Then she sucked on that. She tasted sweet as wine, her mouth hot and welcoming, and I wanted everything in there—my tongue, my cock, my come. I wanted her to taste nothing but me. I had never, ever wanted a woman the way I wanted Tara Montgomery. I could have fucked her until the cops came, fucked her until next week, until we both grew old and died.

I cupped her breast through her shirt, pinched her nipple lightly. She made a sharp sound and ground against me, half-breaking the kiss. "You're going to make me come," she panted against my mouth.

"Not tonight," I said against her lips, rubbing my thumb over her nipple again.

She moaned. "Jace, you're going to kill me."

"Not tonight," I said again. I put both my hands on her hips and moved her back an inch, taking the pressure off.

She slumped her shoulders, her hair dangling, and let out a breath, the tension going out of her body. "Can you at least tell me why?"

"Because you don't want me the way I want you."

She gave a laugh with only a little humor in it. "I thought we wanted each other the same way."

"We do," I said, "and we don't." I ran my thumb over her lower lip one last time because her mouth was the sexiest thing I had ever fucking seen. I let the pad of my thumb drag her lip down, let it run softly over the flesh inside. She turned her face toward my thumb, moving to take it in her mouth again, and I pulled away.

"Go," I told her, not unkindly.

Tara paused for only a second. Then she got off my lap and moved back into the passenger seat. She picked up her purse and opened the passenger door. A second later, it slammed.

And she was gone.

FIFTEEN

Tara

I SHOULD HAVE BEEN mad at him. Insulted. *Was it me?* I should be in a tizzy, calling Jace Riggs names in my head, wondering what was wrong with me that he didn't want me. I should be finished with him. Instead I lay on my bed in my bra and panties, still high from the feel of him. I wasn't mad at all, because we didn't feel finished. I half-dozed and thought about the sensation of his thumb in my mouth, feeling the electricity from that single thought zip up and down my skin, over and over again.

It was late. Midnight, maybe—I didn't really know. I was just drifting off when the phone rang on my nightstand.

I didn't know the number, but somehow I knew who it was. I'd given him my number a few hours ago, after all. "Hello?" I said, answering the phone.

"Okay," Jace said on the other end of the line. "Now that I've beat off in the shower, I suppose I can tell you."

Did he have to turn me on with *everything* he said? I pushed away the visuals in my brain and said, "Tell me what, Jace?"

"I've never had sex."

I went still, unable to say a single word.

"Most people think it's weird," Jace said into the silence. "I get that. But it's true."

I couldn't process this. Not even a little bit. "Never?" I asked.

"I've had the oral kind," he explained bluntly. "Not very often, and not since prison. The other kind, never."

I spent a second unpacking that. My file had said Jace was twenty-five. He'd never had sex with a woman at twenty-five. Though at some point, some girl—more than one—had given him a blow job. The crazy, illogical part of my brain wondered who the fuck those girls were, and whether I could scratch their eyes out. Because, it was time to be honest here, I really wanted that to be me.

"Does that answer your questions?" Jace asked me.

"Not even a little bit," I told him.

He sighed. "Okay, counselor, I'll try. Fire away."

I scrambled, because I had questions. So many questions. I sat up in bed, shivering a little now. "The oral sex," I said. "Was it giving or getting?"

"Both."

That didn't improve the visual. I hated the idea of him with his face between some other woman's legs. "Were you dating these women?"

"No," Jace said. "They were mostly girls who showed up at my brothers' parties. One-time things."

"So you've never had a girlfriend?"

"No, counselor, I haven't."

There was a tinge of resentment in the word *counselor*, Jace with his defenses up, but I could handle that. I talked to people who had their defenses up every day, and I'd certainly butted heads with Jace's defenses more than once. I didn't blame him for feeling vulnerable, telling me this. In fact, it was a miracle he was answering so many questions at all.

"Why?" I asked him. "If you were, um, in a sexual situation with these girls, why didn't you just have sex with them?"

"Because I didn't want to," Jace said.

"That's not an answer."

"I know, but it's the answer I have. I've never wanted to randomly fuck someone I don't know or particularly like. My body might want to, but my brain never has. My brain puts the brakes on every time."

I was tense, my breathing shallow and raspy. My counselor's brain was fired up, but so was my sex brain, and my whole body. I was sitting here in the middle of the night, on my bed in my bra and panties, completely turned on while I tried to analyze Jace Riggs. It was by far the weirdest situation a man had ever put me in.

"I was twenty-three when I went to prison," Jace said to me. "My head's been fucked up since I got out. I can't just introduce myself to a woman and screw her. It's not what I do. And before prison, I was stealing cars and informing on my father for years. I had secrets, a double life. I couldn't date. It was tense, I had to be careful, and I was dealing with a lot of shit. So I could go to a party every once in a while, and sometimes one of the girls there would suck my cock and I'd eat her out. Then I'd go home because I was done. There you go. That's your explanation."

"Okay," I said. What it must have cost him to tell me this. The pure, raw courage it took.

"I didn't want you to think I turned you down because of

you," he said. "That wasn't the reason. That's all I wanted to say. Now go to sleep and forget about me."

"Why?" I asked.

"Because you're better off," he replied. "Good night."

SIXTEEN

Jace

MY BROTHER RYAN showed up at Riggs Auto the next day with his seven-year-old son in tow. I had just finished with a customer's car, and Luke was in the office, wading his way through the numbers shit. I was better at numbers than he was, but Luke was a stubborn ass, and he maintained that he'd never get good at it if he didn't sit in front of the little computer we'd bought and figure it out. So he sat there cursing while I cleaned up in the bay.

I was tired from lack of sleep, but I was used to that. What I wasn't used to was feeling like I'd ripped off my clothes, ripped off my skin, and exposed myself. I felt jagged, uncomfortable. My stomach was in knots and my head buzzed. I worked hard and silent, trying to make the feeling go away.

She knows. Tara knows.

My virginity—fuck, I hated that word, but technically it was true—wasn't something that bothered me every day. It was a thing that bobbed up in my life from time to time, but mostly I tried not to think about it. I knew it was weird for a guy of twenty-five not to have fucked someone. I knew my brothers had very different experiences, and I'd rather die of embarrassment than tell them. I also knew that I needed to take care of it.

Take care of it, like it was an appointment I needed to make to get rid of a rash. But I wasn't leading a double life anymore, and I wasn't in prison anymore. I'd made the decisions I'd made, but I didn't need to head further toward thirty with my lack of experience hanging around my neck.

That, of course, made me think about Tara again.

She probably wasn't interested, but I thought about her anyway. I thought about how she tasted and how she'd felt in my lap. She'd probably back off and go find some experienced guy. If I were her, I would.

"Jay-Cee," Ryan said, giving me a nod as he came in the shop. He liked to try and piss me off by mispronouncing my nickname. His son, Dylan, came in behind Ryan, wearing a Tigers ball cap and an oversized sweatshirt.

"Hey, Uncle Jace," Dylan said, cool as a cucumber. I hadn't seen Dylan since I left for prison, not too long after he'd been dropped on Ryan's doorstep by his grandparents, but the kid took it all in stride, like we saw each other every day.

"Hey, Dylan," I said. "You're a big kid. Better looking than your dad, too."

"Can I see what you're doing?" Dylan asked.

"He loves cars," Ryan said. "It's genetic."

I put Dylan under the car with me and pointed out some stuff. He wanted to look at the engine of the old Mercedes we had parked in one of the bays, so I opened it up and left him to it.

"What are you doing here?" I asked Ryan, wiping my hands with a rag. By now Luke had been drawn out of the office and was sitting in one of the shop's folding chairs. He'd given Dylan a high five, which Dylan, of course, was totally cool with.

Ryan shrugged. "Just decided to get out of the house for a while."

I shared a look with Luke. We Riggs boys weren't all that sociable, especially with each other. We'd grown up in the same house, but we'd fended for ourselves, and we hadn't even liked each other all that much. Ryan, especially, was nowhere near the rest of us.

Ryan had been the Riggs brother who was actually going to go places. He'd been born with good looks and incredible baseball talent, and though Luke, Dex, and I always knew we'd be the kids from the wrong side of the tracks forever, Ryan was going to be something else. Ryan was going to get out. It was easy to hate Ryan for that, but at the same time we secretly hoped he'd make it. At least one of us would get away from Westlake.

He'd almost done it. Almost. Ryan had hit the minor leagues, but he'd never gone further than that. He had a temper and tended to get in fights both on and off the field. Then Dylan appeared three years ago—the four-year-old son Ryan hadn't known he had, who he then had to raise by himself. And finally, last year his shoulder gave out, and he'd been benched for months, going through training and therapy and God knew what else in an effort to get back on the field.

It hadn't worked, at least not yet. Ryan lived in the Detroit suburbs, well over an hour's drive from here in shitty traffic. There was no way he'd just drop in at Riggs Auto. Something was up.

"How is the shop doing?" Ryan asked, leaning back against the car I'd been working on and crossing one ankle over the other. He really was a good-looking asshole—if he hadn't been a baseball phenom, he could have been in movies. Now he was wearing jeans and a flannel shirt, his face clean shaven and his dark brown hair neatly trimmed, and he looked like an underwear model on his day off. He'd been cocky about it in high school, but that cockiness had vanished. Now he watched his son from the corner of his eye, making sure he didn't hurt himself poking in the old Mercedes.

I said nothing, and Luke gave it a long, meaningful pause before he gave a slow drawl of an answer. "The shop," he said, sprawling back on his folding chair, "is doing just fine."

"Good, good," Ryan said. He looked around, somehow still managing to keep the corner of his eye on Dylan—some kind of parenting talent. "You two really cleaned this place up after Dad made a shit show of it."

Our father was in prison for trying to run someone over in his car. That someone was his business partner in the stolen-car enterprise Dad had run through here for years, the one I'd worked for and informed on. We Riggses weren't exactly the Brady Bunch.

But with Dad put away for a long time and the stolen car ring broken up by the cops, Luke and I had decided to make a go of an actual shop—a legitimate one. We'd put in an actual bookkeeping system instead of a bunch of handwritten slips, and we'd gotten a new sign and done some local advertising. We'd hired a couple of employees, casual mechanics who came in a few days a week for now in the hopes that we'd be able to take them on full time. We actually had customers, a small steady trickle so far. The shop's notoriety probably accounted for some of that, but we hoped to win people over with good service.

"We do okay," Luke said. "You just said *shit* in front of Dylan."

"I'm used to it," Dylan said from under the hood.

Ryan shrugged. "He's used to it. So the place is making a profit?"

"What's this about?" I asked him.

Ryan gave me a look from those dark eyes that girls had gone batshit for all through high school. My limited sexual experiences had usually been courtesy of Ryan and the trails of women he left in his wake, though he probably wasn't aware of it. "You're awfully suspicious," he said to me.

"Money," Luke said. "It's definitely about money."

"It isn't about money," Ryan said. He glanced at Dylan. "Okay, it's sort of about money."

Dylan peered around the hood at us. "Dad needs money," he said. "He can't play baseball anymore."

"I thought you were getting the shoulder looked at," I said to Ryan.

Ryan looked pained. He glanced up at the ceiling, then scratched his chin. "The shoulder is toast," he said finally. "It's done."

We were quiet for a second.

"That sucks, man," Luke said.

"Since Dad can't play," Dylan said, "we can't afford the house anymore. Dad says we might have to move. And he needs a job."

Ryan scratched his jaw again. "I raised him to tell the truth," he said. "I'm regretting it at the moment."

"I thought you were doing okay," Luke said. "You said you have a nanny and everything."

Dylan's head popped around the hood again. "Kate's not a nanny. She's a pet sitter."

"She *was* a pet sitter," Ryan said. "Now she takes care of Dylan instead of dogs and cats."

"You hired a nanny with no qualifications?" I asked him.

"She works cheap," Ryan explained, "and Dylan likes her."

"I like her," Dylan agreed.

"Plus, she's hot," Luke said. He grinned at Ryan's expression. "Just a wild guess."

"It's purely professional," Ryan said firmly. Maybe too firmly.

"Kate is pretty," Dylan said. "She has red hair. She constantly has guys calling her for dates."

A muscle in Ryan's jaw twitched. "Why do I take you anywhere?" he asked his son. "At home, I can't get you to say a damn thing."

"Okay, okay," Luke said, cutting in. "Ryan, if you want to come work at Riggs Auto, of course you can." Ryan had learned cars by kindergarten like the rest of us. "It isn't a big-money job, though. We're still rebuilding."

I knew what Luke was thinking. I was thinking the same thing. Ryan was the closest thing to a celebrity that Westlake, and the Riggs brothers, had. To have him working in the garage would probably bring customers—most of them women. I was no marketing expert, but notoriety plus Westlake's almost-famous almost-ex-baseball player was a good way to get traffic.

Ryan nodded. "I'll let you know," he said, like he didn't give a shit. Because he was a Riggs, and we're incapable of saying *Thanks, that's great, I appreciate the help*. It's impossible for us to form the words.

In my pocket, my phone buzzed on silent. I slid it out and saw I had a text. It was Tara.

Don't even try to avoid me after that conversation last night, Riggs. I have questions.

My stomach twisted while I tried not to smile. *You think you can analyze me?* I texted back.

I plan to try, was her immediate response.

"What's this?" Ryan and Dylan were standing at my Thunderbird, and Ryan was walking around it in a circle. "Who brought this awesome piece of metal in?"

"It's mine," I said. "Some guy sold it to Luke for a few hundred bucks. I'm getting it road ready."

Ryan whistled in admiration, and Dylan opened the driver's door to pop the hood. He already looked like he belonged in the shop. Maybe we could use a seven-year-old intern.

My phone buzzed again. *Free therapy session,* Tara said. *Limited time offer.*

Give up, I texted back. *I'm too screwed up.*

So sue me, Tara texted. *I like a challenge.*

I shook my head and ran a hand through my hair. *Okay,* I wrote. *My place. Tonight. See you at eight.*

"Who's that?" I looked up to see Luke watching me texting.

"No one," I said.

Luke opened his mouth to say something, but Ryan interrupted. "Guys."

His voice was deep with alarm. I turned and saw that he'd opened the trunk of my Thunderbird and was staring inside.

"What?" I said. "There's nothing in the trunk. I've looked a hundred times."

In response, Ryan turned to Dylan. "Leave the room, kid."

"I want to see," Dylan protested.

"Nope," Ryan said. "Go in the office and close the door. Give me ten minutes with your uncles. Three, two, one."

Dylan dragged his feet, dying of curiosity, but he went. When the office door had closed behind him, Luke and I walked around the car to see what Ryan was looking at.

He'd pulled up the bottom of the trunk, opening up the space where the spare tire was kept. I'd never looked in there; I hadn't had time. Now I saw that inside the space, there was no spare tire at all. Instead, there was something else.

"Oh, shit," Luke said.

A cold sweat broke out on the back of my neck and I felt bile in my throat. "You have got to be fucking kidding me," I said, my voice a croak.

Set deep inside the wheel well were six neatly wrapped packages of white powder.

I was an ex-con, I'd just finished parole two days ago, and I had six kilos of coke in my car.

We were silent for a minute while I quietly tried not to throw up.

"Okay," Ryan said, running a hand through his hair. "We can fix this. We can."

"It's six kilos of coke," I said. "You don't fucking fix it, Ryan. You get rid of it. Now."

"You have to get rid of it right," Luke pointed out. He looked pretty green too, since he was the one who'd bought the car, and he co-owned the shop where this shit was currently sitting. "You don't just throw it in the trash or something. And where the fuck did it come from? What if someone is looking for it?"

I scrubbed both hands over my face. "Jesus. Okay. Okay. I'm not panicking. What do we do?"

Ryan sighed. "I hate to say it, but there's one guy who will know exactly what to do with this. And I mean exactly."

I groaned. I knew exactly who Ryan meant. "He's a loose cannon. Who knows what the fuck he'll do?"

"Ryan is right," Luke said. "He can fix this. He's the only one we know who can do it right. So who's going to call him?"

I dropped my hands and pulled my phone from my pocket. "Fine," I said. "Jesus Christ, what a mess. I'll do it. I'll be the one to call Dex."

SEVENTEEN

Jace

DEX STARED into the wheel well of my car for a long time, his expression unreadable.

"Okay, Jace," he said at last. "You have a fucking problem."

Dex was the oldest of us, which wasn't saying much—Dex and Ryan had different mothers, so they were only four months apart. Dex had spent time as a cop on the Detroit PD before he'd resigned—some rumors said he'd had a nervous breakdown and couldn't hack the job, while other rumors said there were corruption charges coming down the pipeline, so Dex had gotten out while the getting was good. No one knew the truth, and Dex wasn't saying anything because Dex was batshit crazy.

He'd always been crazy. He was the brother who took jumps off the side of the quarry into the shallow water or tried to flip his bike off a ramp. As an adult, he still had the same mentality. No one ever knew what Dex would do. Which, I had to admit, made him almost perfect for this situation.

He stood up straight right now and took a joint from his pocket. "Helps me think," he said when Ryan glared at him. We let him light up because Dylan wasn't in the shop anymore. Luke had called in Emily, and she'd taken Dylan to the movies, a worried look on her face. I knew exactly how she felt.

Dex puffed the joint, thinking. "Okay," he said through the smoke. "First off, where the fuck did this car come from?"

"A guy sold it to me," Luke said.

"This guy have a name?"

"He said his name was Richard Wagner. He said the paperwork would come next week."

"So a fake name, then," Dex said. "Well done. If he'd said his name was Chuck Norris, would you have believed him?"

"Bite me, Dex," Luke said.

"Noted." Dex took another draw on the joint. He needed a haircut, and his dark hair was haphazardly shoved back from his forehead, tousled. His flannel shirt was rumpled and his well-worn jeans hung low on his hips. Dex was a poster boy for the sort-of-homeless look; for all I knew, he actually was homeless, since I didn't know where he lived. How he'd ever gotten through the police academy was a mystery to us all, but his disintegration afterward was pretty much total.

"That's definitely coke," Dex said, "in case there was any doubt. The packages have cartel stamps on them. That's bad fucking news. Was this Richard Wagner Hispanic?"

"No, he was a white guy," Luke said. "He said it was his dad's car, and his dad just died. He didn't want it, so he sold it to me."

"I've been working on it," I said. "I can vouch that it hasn't been driven in months. The tires were flat, the shocks were shot. Rust everywhere."

"So it wasn't driven over the border and all the way to Michigan," Dex said. "At least, not recently. Which means the coke was stuffed in there from somewhere else."

"Or it was driven over the border a long time ago," I pointed out.

"Maybe dear old Pops did it. Stole cartel coke and had to stash it." Dex looked thoughtful. He took another toke, then ground out his joint. "Then he croaked. Inconvenient, but the theory works. It's possible the cartel doesn't even know where their coke is." He looked at me. "You have four options, Jace. One, you can sell this. Two, you can snort it. Three, you call the cops. And four, you dump it. Let's start with number one. This shit is worth a lot of money—enough to set you up. I probably know guys who can move it. But it will get you arrested if you're lucky, killed if you aren't."

I stared at him. "Are you fucking kidding me? Dex, you were a *cop*."

"Who do you think cops meet all day every day, Jace? I was vice. You think I was arresting jaywalkers? The guys I dealt with were the guys who move stuff like this."

I pinched the bridge of my nose. "I am not selling coke."

"Fine then, option two. It goes up your nose. It would take a while, this much. Nifty way to dispose of it."

"Fuck off. No. Next."

"Just checking. Next, you call the Westlake PD and tell them the truth. That some guy sold you this car with coke in it. That you're totally innocent, and you are in no way dealing drugs through Riggs Auto, where Dad ran a stolen car ring for years and probably dealt whatever he could get his hands on."

I felt my stomach twist, and I dropped my hand. "You're saying they won't believe me."

"You're a con, Jace," Dex said. "You think they're going to believe you?"

Luke broke in. "Emily's mother is a cop. She's not evil, and she's not stupid. She'd hear you out, investigate it the right way."

"With what outcome?" Dex looked around at us. "Sure, she'd listen, but what would the cops decide? Riggs Auto is dirty. It's been dirty for years. Dad is dirty, and everyone thinks we are too."

"Bullshit," Luke argued. "Emily's mother doesn't think that."

"She changed her mind, what, a month ago?" Ryan said. "When you and Emily got together? Before that she thought we were scum, just like everyone else does."

"Besides," I said, "Emily's mother doesn't have the final say. There will be an investigation with me in the middle of it. This"—I pointed to the trunk of my car—"is hard time. *Federal* time. If I go down, I go all the way down and I never come up again. I'm supposed to risk that because you've been to Sunday dinner at Emily's a few times?"

"You bought the car, Luke," Ryan added. "It's sitting in Riggs Auto right now. If Riggs Auto gets shut down, what do we do then?"

Dex held up a hand. "I think we can all agree that we are all royally fucked, Jace especially, if the cops take this. So that leaves option four. We ghost this shit. If it's gone, it never happened."

I scrubbed a hand through my hair. The sooner the stuff was gone, the better. "Do we dump it in the sewer?" I asked.

"Too risky," Dex said.

"Toss it in the quarry?" Ryan said.

Dex tutted. "Jesus, Mickey Mantle. Come up with something better than that."

"Take it to the dump," Luke suggested.

Dex pointed at him. "Close. But not quite. I'm going to need a few supplies. At dusk, we get this done."

CASEY SIMPSON RAN a junkyard outside the Westlake city limits, a few acres of scrubby land he'd put a fence around. People paid him to dump their shit in there, and in return for asking no questions, Casey reserved the right to scavenge whatever he decided was worthwhile.

Casey lived in a shack fifty feet from the yard's gated entrance, where he mostly spent his days drinking himself into oblivion. He started around ten a.m., and by five or six he was usually passed out, at which point getting into the junkyard was fair game. You just had to know the tricks.

Dex knew the tricks, of course. Why would a Riggs boy go to school when he could learn this stuff instead?

At six o'clock, Ryan did a circuit of Casey's house on foot, checking through the window that Casey was out cold. When he gave the signal, I climbed the fence at the yard's southwest corner, where one of the overgrown trees blocked the view of the security camera. I balanced myself on top of the fence and unhooked the wires from the blocked camera, which shut down the feed through every camera on the circuit. It was a stupid way to wire it, but Casey had done the wiring himself, and he was a shitty electrician.

With the cameras out, I gave the signal to Luke and climbed off the fence again. Luke climbed the fence near the front guardhouse, which was empty, and jumped onto the roof. He slid down, went into the guardhouse, and shut off the alarm. He also opened the electronic lock for the front gate, which left only the gate's huge padlock in effect.

I jogged down Route Seven a quarter mile away from Casey's place and got in the tow truck we'd left parked there. By the time I got to the yard's gate, Dex had finished picking the padlock and was swinging the gate open. I got out of the tow, unhooked the Thunderbird, and Ryan got behind the wheel of the car as I pushed it.

Dex and Luke joined me. We pushed the car—my car—into the yard in silence as dark fell, the lights off, the engine dead. No one said anything. Maybe I was emotional, but to me it felt like a funeral.

We kept pushing as Ryan steered, heading for the north section of the yard. Sweat was trickling down my back beneath my black hoodie.

"You couldn't have fixed the engine?" Luke grunted to me as we pushed.

"It would have made too much noise, dickface," Dex grunted back.

"Casey's out cold," Luke said, his arms straining. "He wouldn't hear if we drove a monster truck through here."

"Shut up, both of you," I said as sweat rolled down my temples. "We're almost there."

The north part of the yard had other cars in it—junkers that didn't run, dropped off to Casey over the years. They were in various states of rust, from an old pickup that looked like it was disintegrating to a wheelless Volvo that looked relatively new. We grunted and pushed the Thunderbird toward them.

When we finally got there, we stopped pushing and Ryan got out of the car. "Nice work, suckers," he said, grinning at us. "Too bad I have this bum shoulder or I totally would have helped."

"You're an asshole," I said, using my sleeve to mop my brow.

"We couldn't have left it in another part of the lot?" Luke asked Dex, stretching his back.

"No. Jesus. It's like I didn't teach you guys a fucking thing," Dex said, popping the Thunderbird's trunk and taking his supplies out.

"You didn't," I said.

"Well, I'm teaching you now. Watch the master at work." He pulled out a wad of rags and tossed us each one. "Wipe," he told us. "Don't miss an inch."

We wiped the car down—every surface, everywhere any one of us might have touched. I even opened the hood and wiped down the engine, since I'd worked on it, while Luke got on his back under the car and wiped the undercarriage. Dex snapped rubber gloves on, lifted a sharp piece of metal from a nearby junk pile, and used it to cut careful slits into each of the kilos of coke, letting them fall open.

Next he pulled out gas cans. "Luke," he said, tossing him one. "Over there." He pointed to the cars on the left. "Ryan, over there." He tossed Ryan a can and pointed to the cars on the right.

"We're torching everything?" Ryan said.

"This seems like overkill," I pointed out.

Dex looked at me. "Jace, the car has to go. It was used to either transport the coke, store it, or both. We don't know who's looking for it, who's marked it. It has to go."

I closed my eyes. "I know."

"If we burn one car—just one—what are the cops going to look at?" Dex said. "*That one car*. If we burn five or six cars in the back of a junkyard and make a big-ass fire, the cops have to look at the whole thing, which takes days, and it looks more like an accident or a couple of asshole kids fooling around. Believe me, no PD is going to waste a lot of resources sifting through the burned-out junk in Casey's yard, trying to figure out if there's something important in it."

"You're sure the coke will burn?" I asked him.

Dex held up his own gas can and poured gasoline into the wheel well. "Trust me, it will fucking burn."

So we did it. I sprinted back through the yard toward the gate and the tow truck as Dex pulled out his matches and Ryan and Luke ran for the back fence. I had just gone through the gate when the fire went up behind me in a big *whoosh* of heat and flame. I swung into the tow truck and drove it down a back road, out of sight of Casey's shack when he inevitably woke up in the next few minutes. By the time Casey looked groggily out his window, wondering what the commotion was, there would be nothing but fire and no sign of a Riggs brother anywhere.

It was wrong. We were damaging property, covering up a crime, destroying evidence, and torching my car. As an ex-con, I should have been doing exactly none of those things. Every single one of them was a risk.

And damn it, I thought as I bumped the truck over the service road, it was fun.

I cut the engine on the tow in the dark, looking at the glow of the fire half a mile away. Dex was the first one to reach the truck, opening the passenger door and climbing in next to me. He already had a lit joint between his lips.

He gave me a Dex grin, the corner of his mouth twisting up over the joint. His face was mood-lit in the dark, his hair mussed, his jaw unshaven. Dex was good-looking, but the girls who went for him were always a little suicidal. "You really are a Riggs after all," he said to me.

"You had a doubt?" I asked him.

"All those years stealing cars and informing on Dad at the same time," Dex said. "I could look at you all day and still not know what's in your fucking head."

I stared at him, ice cold creeping up the back of my neck.

Dex shook his head, took the joint between his fingers. "Come on, Jace," he said. "I'm a cop."

"Not anymore." The words came out harsh because I was shocked and horrified. Dex knew. He *knew*.

"I'm cop enough to figure out a few simple things," Dex said. "Like you hate Dad as much as I do, so there was no way you were spending your life as his little bitch. Which meant you were lying."

My body was clammy with panic. I looked at Dex and wondered if he was thinking about the time I'd asked for a bike—if he even remembered that day. "Dex," I said, "no one can know. I mean no one. If—"

"I've known almost from the beginning, and I didn't spill," Dex said. "You think I'm going to spill on you now and get you killed? Here comes Ryan."

I tried to unclench my jaw, dig my fingernails out of my icy palms. The entire escapade tonight—the break-in, the fire, the coke—didn't scare me as much as what Dex had just told me. The information I'd passed had taken down some very powerful people—people who thought nothing of killing not only me, but everyone around me. My brothers. Tara. If the men I'd informed on knew who I was, they would kill Tara in a heartbeat.

The back door opened and Ryan swung into the truck. "Whoee," he said, "we haven't done anything like that since high school. Remember the time we took down all the basketball hoops in the park and put them on the freeway?"

I did. That had been fun. You should never leave basketball hoops that aren't cemented down when there are Riggs brothers around. It's your own fault, really.

The other back door opened and Luke got in. "Let's move," he said. "Emily just texted me. She took Dylan for a movie and a snack, but now they're both curious about what we're doing."

I turned the key in the ignition as Dex said, "Luke, you have an old lady now. What are you going to tell her?"

"I'll tell her the truth," Luke said. "I'll just tell her after we've already gotten away with it, so she can yell all she wants. Also, if I want to keep my balls I'll never refer to her as an old lady."

"I'm not telling Dylan," Ryan said. "He's only seven. I'm supposed to be normal dad. I don't want him getting ideas."

"Role model, huh?" Dex said, laughing.

"Fuck you, Dex," Ryan said. "Someday you'll have a kid, and all you'll want is to be boring." He sighed and looked out the window, running a hand through his perfect hair. "Damn, though, that *was* fun."

He sounded sad about it. I knew exactly how he felt.

EIGHTEEN

Tara

I HADN'T TOLD Jace what I was doing on my Saturday off, and he hadn't asked. For once, was glad for his stubborn sealed-off ways. There was no one in the world who was less nosy than Jace Riggs, and today it worked to my benefit.

I took a cab to get my car and headed to Westlake's north end, where they were building the new subdivisions. Maybe it was hopeful of the town to develop them, but Westlake had a nice middle-class population if you were on the right side of the tracks. That population was growing, and some of them were buying the new houses in town.

I left streets that had big old trees and drove down brand-new roads, the houses with no grass or fresh sod laid down, some of the sites still piled with machinery and dirt. These weren't going to be mansions; they were small, modest places, mostly townhouses, for young couples to live in as they moved their way up. I knew, because until eight months ago I was going to live in one myself.

Kyle still lived in the house we'd bought. It was his house now —he'd paid me my half of the down payment and taken over the mortgage. He said he liked the place, he could afford it, and he didn't want to leave. That was fine with me, so I'd packed my things and moved into my little rental.

I pulled into the driveway—Kyle's SUV was there, so he was home, just like we'd arranged—and pulled some empty boxes from my trunk. Then I mounted the front porch steps and rang the doorbell.

He opened the door almost immediately; he'd probably been waiting. He was wearing jeans and a pullover sweatshirt—his day-off wear. It was rare for Kyle not to be on shift on a Saturday, and for a second I remembered how well I used to know his schedule.

"Hey," he said. He had showered, shaved. He was a nice-looking guy, and he was strong and fit because of his job. He made good money and now had a nice house. By any definition, he was a catch.

"Hi," I said to him. I held up the boxes. "Thanks for letting me in. I won't take long."

"Sure," he said. He stepped aside to let me in, and I walked upstairs, ready to collect the last few things I hadn't been able to grab when I moved out. I was halfway down the upstairs hall when it dawned on me that the stuff I needed was in the dresser and the closet in the bedroom. Kyle's bedroom, formerly our bedroom. And he was following me down the hall.

I shook it off. It didn't matter; we were over. We'd been over for a long time. I was not going back to Kyle, and nothing was going to happen in that bedroom. I just had to get this over with and go.

You're being too nice about him, said Jace's voice in my head.

He should never have fucked you if you didn't like it, if you had to fake it.

And then: *I've never had sex.*

I wouldn't think about that right now. I wouldn't.

"How have you been?" Kyle asked as I entered the bedroom and put my boxes down.

"Good, thanks," I said, opening a drawer of the dresser that used to be mine.

"You look good."

"Thank you," I said again. "How is the job?" Because maybe if we were chatting, it would be easier for neither of us to look at the bed. I was definitely not looking at the bed.

"The same," Kyle said. "It's a mess. It always is."

I nodded, pulling sweaters from a drawer and putting them in a box.

"I haven't touched anything," Kyle said.

"Okay."

"Tara."

I turned and looked at him, but he shook his head. "I know that look," he said. "Your determined look. Nothing's going to get you talking, is it?"

I shoved more sweaters in the box. Why did I have so many freaking sweaters? "There's nothing to talk about. We did all of our talking months ago."

"I'm on a bunch of dating sites now."

That should have at least made me flinch, but it didn't. I moved to the closet and pulled more clothes from a shelf.

From behind me, Kyle said, "You know what I found? It's easy to get laid, but it's harder to find someone to talk to."

This I recognized. When things had fallen apart at the end, when Kyle realized he didn't have control of the situation or of me, he'd resorted to nastiness. Things that were supposed to hurt me. His talking about sleeping with other women was supposed to hurt me. What he didn't understand was that it only made me want to get this over with sooner.

"I don't even need the websites, really," Kyle continued. "You know there have always been women hanging around guys like me. We attract them like groupies. There are times I can just take my pick."

This was terrible. Not because what he said broke my heart, but because I could feel my whole body clench. I never wanted this man to touch me again. I'd felt that way before last night, but now—after Jace Riggs had had his hands and his mouth and his tongue on me—the thought made me want to shudder. The difference between the two men could not be more clear: Kyle with his self-involved crap, and Jace with those damn eyes that saw everything.

Kyle was waiting for me to say something, so I gritted out, "That's nice."

"It isn't like your job, is it?" Kyle said. "The only men you meet are John the middle-aged bore and the scum that come to your sessions. Though don't get me wrong—I bet John would fuck you. You'd just have to ask him nicely."

He was trying to make me angry now, trying to get me to hurl insults back at him, trying to make me fight and hurt. Provocation was one thing Kyle was very, very good at. He saw it every day in his job, just like I did.

"I'm done," I said, stacking the boxes and carrying them toward the bedroom door. They were awkward, though not heavy, and I had to peer around them to aim for the door frame. I stopped when I felt Kyle's hand on my arm.

I froze. In all of our arguments, in the nasty fragments of our relationship, he'd never hurt me, never even grabbed me. Even now his touch was almost tentative, not a hard grip. And still, it made me shiver.

"Seriously, Tara, what are you going to do?" he said. "Become an old spinster? Maybe find some ugly loser ex-con to service you?"

He knew nothing about Jace Riggs. *Nothing.* But this was Kyle's superpower: shooting enough ugly barbs at you until one of them hit. No wonder the divorce rate in men of his profession was sky-high.

"What I do is none of your business," I said, "and leave my clients out of it."

He was quiet for a second as I made my way down the hall. He didn't offer to help, of course. As I started down the stairs he said, "If I hear you're dating anyone from the force, he's going to have a big fucking problem. And so are you."

So that was what he was worried about. "Not a chance," I shouted back, and walked out the front door to load my car.

I drove three blocks and pulled over at a half-built lot, dirt under my tires. My hands were shaking and I needed to see Jace so bad it almost turned my stomach. I pulled out my phone and composed a text that sounded lighthearted, not like I was desperate for a glimpse of him. *Don't even try to avoid me after that conversation last night, Riggs. I have questions.*

You think you can analyze me? he texted back.

I plan to try.

I stared out the window and felt the burn in my chest. And I wondered how I was going to tell the man I was falling for that my ex-boyfriend was a cop on the Westlake PD.

NINETEEN

Tara

AT EIGHT O'CLOCK I pulled into the driveway of the Riggs house. The sun had almost finished setting, leaving a rosy glow on the horizon and deep shadows beneath the trees. In the main house, a single light was lit in an upstairs window. There was another light in the window of the guest house, which I could see when I got out of the car.

I'd dropped off my boxes at my apartment. I'd had something to eat and changed into a simple cotton sundress of deep red with a pattern of dark blue and green leaves. I wore flat sandals, almost no makeup, and my hair was down, clean and brushed, falling down my back. A casual late-summer outfit. Carefully chosen for meeting the hot virgin ex-con former client who I was a little bit obsessed with and hoped to either analyze or devirginize—or, if I was lucky, maybe both.

My stomach was still twisted when I knocked on the guest

house door, the aftereffect of the encounter with Kyle. Then the door opened and Jace was there, and the sour feeling turned into a twist of pure crazy anticipation, deep in my gut, up my spine, and between my legs.

He was wearing jeans and a white T-shirt that had a smear of something black on it—grease, maybe. His hair was mussed and his eyes were a little wild. "Shit," he said. "It's eight already, isn't it? I just got back."

"From where?"

He scrubbed a hand through his hair, making it stick up more. "My brothers..." He trailed off. "Never mind. I was going to take a shower. I didn't have time. I don't think I smell good."

"Is this a bad time?" I asked.

"No, no. Shit."

He was so flustered, it was kind of adorable. "Okay then, if it isn't a bad time, are you going to let me in?"

He seemed to take this question seriously. "Yeah, I am." He stepped back, but he also curled his hand lightly around my upper arm, as if he thought I would go running off. "Sorry. Come in."

I let him lead me into the guest house. I was distracted by his arms—I'd never seen him in short sleeves before. He'd always worn a jacket or a hoodie. He had tattoos down both arms, coming from under his sleeves and snaking down his forearms. There was ink on the soft skin of the inside of one bicep. I hadn't known that about Jace, that he had tattoos. *Good lord.* The anticipation twisted harder.

He didn't seem to notice my lust-filled silence. "Just have a seat or something," he said. "I meant to clean up in here."

I brushed closer to him and caught a sharp smell. Oil, the tang of sweat, and possibly gasoline. "It's okay," I said. "If you want to take a shower, go ahead. I'll wait."

He paused and looked at me. Those gray eyes, those dark lashes. He was uncertain about something, I could see that. I wondered if it was me or something else. I wondered if he could see the uncertainty in my own eyes—uncertainty about Kyle, about myself, about whether I should even be here. Even though, if I admitted the truth to myself, there was nowhere else I wanted to be.

As if he was reading my mind, Jace said, "What are we doing, Tara?"

"Talking," I replied. "If you want."

His gaze dropped to my neck, my collarbones, then rose back to my face, and for a second his eyes grew dark. *You don't want me the way I want you,* he'd said. Right now the air between us was about to catch fire. I stood there and let it sizzle, let him decide.

He took a breath and rubbed a hand over his jaw. He was wearing his rings, and I realized I wanted him to be wearing his rings when he put his fingers inside me. I was shocked and turned on at my own thought.

"You want a drink?" Jace said.

"Okay," I managed.

He turned away, and I looked around for the first time. The guest house was actually rather nice—a little like a hotel suite. The main room had a big bed in it, neatly made, with a simple plaid coverlet. A small table and two chairs. A door leading to a bathroom on the other side of the room. On this side, near the front door, a corner of kitchen, with a sink, a fridge, a small stove, and a coffeemaker. It wasn't much, but I imagined for a man who'd spent twenty months in a cell with no privacy, it was luxurious.

There was a well-used laptop sitting on the small table beneath a stack of books. There were more books next to the bed, and still more on the kitchen counter. A small TV sat in one corner, but since it had books piled in front of it, it didn't look like it got used much.

While Jace opened two beers he had in the fridge, I looked at the book nearest me, which was pressed open against the counter, like he was midway through reading it. It was Dostoevsky's *Crime and Punishment*.

Jace caught me reading the title, and I smiled at him. "Light reading?"

He shrugged and handed my beer to me. "It was fifty cents at a library sale, and I like to read classics."

"Is it good?"

"It's hard to understand, and the language is complicated, and everyone's name seems the same," he said. "But I keep at it. I like a challenge, and it's better than TV."

I sipped my beer and smiled at him.

"What?" Jace said.

"You're complicated and hard to understand," I said. "And a challenge."

His eyes widened. "A come-on line," he said, pleased. "I knew it. I thought you just wanted to talk, counselor."

I felt myself grinning. "It was pretty good, wasn't it?"

"Not bad," he said. "Have a seat."

I took my beer and sat in one of the chairs. The bed sat in the middle of the room, basically shouting at us, but Jace didn't seem to notice. He sat on the edge of the bed and untied his boots. "Sorry," he said, glancing up at me. "Long day."

"Really, I can come back."

"Quit it." He kicked the boots off. "You said you had questions. Ask away."

"Okay." I ran my fingers over the lip of my beer bottle. Jace put his elbows on his knees, letting his hands dangle between them, and watched me. I realized that this setup was a little like counseling—the two of us sitting across from each other, me asking questions. He wasn't my client anymore, and we were in his home—his bedroom—and we were on the edge of pushing our relationship into sex. But still, this setup was the one he was used to, the one we were both used to in a way. So I relaxed my shoulders and went with it.

"I've been thinking about what you told me," I said, "about your lack of sexual experience."

He rolled his eyes—there were those familiar Jace defenses. But to his credit, he didn't shut me down. "Go on."

"Well, it seems to me that sex is only the surface issue. The deeper issue is intimacy."

"As in?"

"As in, you have a problem with it."

He laughed, not seeming to notice that I went thick with lust at the sound, at the way his face relaxed when he did it. "I guess I'd have a problem with it if I'd ever had any," he said.

"That's what I mean. Your mother left when you were very young, and your father was a terrible parent. Your brothers weren't any help, though they're older."

"They were too busy surviving on their own," he said.

"Fair enough. But that left you alone."

"Plenty of people who are alone do a lot of fucking," Jace pointed out.

I nodded agreement. "But that's how they express, however unsatisfyingly, their desire to be close to another person, even for a short time. And that isn't how you do it."

"So how do I do it?"

"I don't know," I said. "You tell me."

He didn't even think about it. He reached down and took my heel in his hand, lifting my foot up. He slid my sandal off. "I do it by arguing with my counselor," he said. "By going to her office and sitting on the bench outside. By harassing her."

"You're not harassing me," I said, outraged on his behalf. I couldn't take my eyes from the sight of his hands on my skin, those beautiful fingers, those sexy rings. "I like it."

"Good," he said, putting one foot down and lifting the other. He took the other sandal off and let his hand wander smoothly up the back of my bare calf. "Okay, we've analyzed me," he said. "Let's analyze you."

His hand on my leg was obscene. I was wet, my pussy pounding with pressure, and I was also crazily glad I'd shaved my legs this afternoon. "What about me?"

"Your intimacy problem," Jace said, his gaze also on his hand as it moved.

"I don't..." I had to stop talking when his fingers traced the soft skin behind my knee. "...have one."

"Sure you do." He was so quietly confident, so self-assured. He lifted his hand from my leg and took my elbow instead, tugging me from the chair and over to sit on the bed. He stood in front of me, all six feet plus of him, muscle and motor oil and masculine perfection. He touched the side of my face, traced a finger over my lower lip. "You said you didn't like fucking the last guy you were with."

"I..." Had I said that? My mind was blank. "I didn't like it," I said, thinking of what it had felt like to have Kyle touch me, be inside me. Of the times I'd cried silently in the bathroom afterward, thinking there was something wrong with me.

"You lived with him," Jace said, kneeling—actually getting on his knees in front of me. "And you hated fucking him." His hands moved up beneath the skirt of my dress, his fingers hooking into the waist of my panties, tugging them. "That left you alone. All alone."

"Jace," I said, but I lifted my hips so he could pull my panties off. He drew them down my legs and threw them away.

He put his hands on my knees and parted them, though the hem of my dress sagged down and still covered me. He lifted his gray gaze to mine and held it. "You fuck anyone else since him, Tara?"

I couldn't look away from him. "No," I breathed.

He moved his hands up under my dress, parting my thighs wider. "I didn't think so," he said. "Heal thyself, counselor." And he dipped his face between my legs.

I made a mewling sound, and it was so good, *so good,* that I dropped back onto my elbows on the bed so he could have better access. Jace parted my pussy lips, found my clit, and licked it soundly while kneeling on the floor. Everything inside me went haywire as his beard scraped the skin of my inner thighs and his tongue slid down, into me, then out and up to my clit again. My legs jerked, and Jace held them, and he sucked my clit softly, and just like that I came, the orgasm a rush that made me feel relief and an edge of deeper want at the same time. I pulsed my hips up against his mouth and then flopped fully back onto the bed.

"Oh, my god," I panted.

Jace took his mouth off me and pushed my dress up, past my waist, his touch a little rough. I took over and pulled the dress the rest of the way off as he bent and kissed my lower belly, my hipbones, his hands holding me still as he worked his way up to my breasts. I unclasped my bra and tossed it away. I had barely a second to wonder if I should be self-conscious about my small breasts before he lowered his mouth to one nipple.

I moaned again, arching up into him. My nipples had always been painfully sensitive, something he seemed to instinctively know. I yanked at his T-shirt, and he reared up briefly to rip it off. I had a glimpse of his muscled shoulders, the sleek ink of his tattoos on his warm skin, before he bent down and took my other nipple in his mouth.

I ran my hands over his arms, his biceps, his shoulder blades, the muscles of his back. I touched his soft hair and the back of his neck as he released my nipple and kissed upward, moving until he was fully over me. Then I ran my hand down the side of his body to his hip and I cupped him through his jeans—his hard cock, his balls. I curled my fingers over it and rubbed my palm on it as he moaned against my skin, his hot breath on my neck.

"You're not my type," I breathed, cupping him harder.

His tattooed arms were tense, holding him over me. "I know," he said against me, his beard scratching me. "We're a terrible idea. You want to fuck me, counselor?"

He'd called me that in defense, and in friendship, but when he said it now it was unbearably hot. "Yes," I said.

"Good. I want to fuck you, too. I have since we first met." He eased up and kissed my mouth, deep and needy yet gentle, his tongue tasting every part of me. I kissed him back, let him inside my mouth as I undid the buttons of his jeans and worked my hand inside them, tracing his cock through his boxer briefs.

He broke the kiss, scraping his teeth on my lip. We were both panting like teens in the backseat of a car. "Fuck, I want to be inside you," he said.

I rubbed him harder. He felt big, and I'd never wanted anything so much in my life. "Tell me you have a condom," I breathed.

"Found some in the bathroom. Probably from my brothers." He seemed to have lost the ability to make complete sentences. He pushed off me—I extracted my hand from inside his jeans—and stumbled to the bathroom in the dark. I heard him bang around in there, and then he came back as I sat up and scooted to the edge of the bed again, naked now.

He stood in front of me, and I yanked at the waist of his jeans. "Off," I told him, impatient. He handed me the strip of condoms and I pulled one off, unwrapping it as he pushed his jeans and boxer briefs to the floor. Then he stood in front of me naked, his cock out and ready for me. I took it in my hand and put the crown in my mouth, unable to help myself.

Jace made a strangled sound. "Tara."

He tasted good. I pushed his cock further into my mouth, taking in its outlines with my tongue, tracing its contours. He was big and thick, just like I'd imagined. Because yes, I'd imagined Jace's cock. Multiple times.

He hissed a breath. "Tara," he warned again.

He was right. I wanted him inside me, right now. I drew back and unrolled the condom over him, sliding it down to the base, then stroking his balls as I kissed his hip.

With a growl he pushed me back on the bed, and then he was there with me, his big body against mine, his hard thigh between mine, his hands tangling in my hair. He kissed me quick and deep, his mouth hard on mine. "You like that?" he asked. "My cock?"

"Yes," I said, because I did. I did.

"Then fuck me," he ordered.

He rolled on his back. I straddled him and he leaned back, letting me get in position. From here I could see the smattering of dark hair on his chest, the shadowed curl of his stomach muscles. I could see the landscape of his pecs and his gorgeous shoulders. I very much liked this view.

I positioned myself over him, put the head of his cock against me, and sunk down. Jace groaned and gripped one hip with his hands, his muscles straining with tension. I sunk further—I was wet, and so ready after an orgasm, but still I could feel him stretching me, pushing me apart. I panted in pleasure, gripping him with my knees.

"Fuck," he said, pushing his hips up, penetrating me harder. My muscles relaxed and I took him, all the way, until he was finally fully in. I felt full, and a rush of possessiveness came over me for the cock inside me. *Mine,* I thought. *Mine.*

I rocked on him, and Jace pushed himself up on his arms, taking the back of my head roughly with one hand. His mouth came on mine, and we began, me moving my hips, him pushing up into me, his mouth scraping mine, his tongue inside me. "Fuck me how you like," he said on an exhale, and I closed my eyes and rocked harder, letting him take me. I was lost. I didn't even feel like myself, recognize myself. I just pushed myself onto him over and over, claiming him, chasing another orgasm.

Already I was close, so close. I pulled my mouth from his. "Your fingers," I said, moving on him. "I need them. Please."

He moved his fingers between us, stroking me. "There?" he asked softly.

"Oh." My head fell back.

Jace moved his fingers. "There."

That was the spot. I rocked harder still, moving my hips to get the most of his fingertips, not caring that we were sweating and the bed was rocking. This was mine. No woman would ever have this, this piece of this particular extraordinary man. This was mine, all mine, and I wanted to come, and I wanted him to come. I dug my fingers into the hard flesh of his shoulders.

He wound his free hand in my hair again, hard, his mouth coming to my ear. "I knew it," he said in his sexy low voice as he stroked me with his cock and his fingers. "I knew you'd fuck like this. I knew you'd be so dirty for me. My smart-mouthed counselor. I wanted to be inside you. I wanted your legs spread. I fucking wanted to watch you come."

I came apart, my body pulsing with another orgasm as I cried out. I felt myself squeezing him, rippling over his cock, and Jace thrust up into me hard, losing control. He pounded me from below, all of his strength drilling into me, and I took it, my body absorbing the shock. Then he let out a cry of his own and I felt him start to pulse.

He flipped me roughly onto my back without disconnecting and shoved into me that way, still pulsing, still coming, his body arching over mine. After what seemed like an eternity he started to relax, his body settling over mine, warm and sticky with sweat. We were still joined. I wrapped my legs around his waist and locked my ankles.

We lay there for a minute, unable to speak, unable to think. I thought, maybe, that I had never been so happy in my life. That had been *spectacular*. I felt fully, completely alive.

Still, Jace was a big man. I unlocked my ankles and pushed his shoulder. "You're crushing me," I said.

He turned his face into my neck. "I can die like this," he said. "This is perfect. Right here."

I smiled and pushed him again. "Don't die, please."

"I could go right now and have no complaints," he said, but he pushed his weight up onto his arms. He leaned in and kissed me softly on the mouth, the touch strangely sweet.

He broke away and looked down to where we were still joined. "I should..." He pulled out of me, then looked at me. "Do you... need anything?"

Because, of course, he hadn't done this before. I felt my chest squeeze. "No," I said. "I'm fine."

He swung off the bed and walked to the bathroom. And left me staring at the ceiling, wondering what the hell I was going to do. Because I wasn't falling for him anymore. I had fallen.

And I had a feeling I still had further to go.

TWENTY

Jace

SHE WAS SITTING cross-legged on the bed, wearing my T-shirt. The white one with a smear of motor oil on it that I'd discarded on the floor. Her long brown hair was twisted and tousled down her back, her legs slender and graceful beneath the hem of the shirt, her feet delicate and perfect.

I was sitting up in bed, next to her, leaning on pillows against the headboard. I wore the sheet up to my waist and nothing else. I had one arm propped behind my head and the other resting on my stomach. If you'd offered to pay me a million dollars to move from that exact spot, I'd have told you no.

"I think we should talk," Tara said.

"Why am I not surprised?" I asked.

She watched my face and then she smiled, just enough that I knew she caught my teasing. "I'm serious."

"I know."

"This," she said, pointing to herself and me and back again. "This, here. We need to be clear about what it is."

Of course she'd be direct. She asked everything head-on. It was what I liked about her. I felt a second of aching fear because she had no idea how I felt about her. None. "You think it was a one-time thing?" I asked her.

"I hope it isn't," she said.

My stomach dropped at that. It was something, at least. A start. "Yeah, well, I was hoping you'd get dressed and leave," I said. "I'd like to set up my Tinder account."

"Shut up," she said, the words with no sting in them. "Nice try. I'm not going anywhere."

There it was. Our gazes locked for a long minute. *No,* I thought. *You're not going anywhere.*

"What?" she said to me. "You're looking at me funny."

"Am I?" We were back to fencing.

"Tell me the truth, Jace Riggs. I can't read your mind."

I rubbed my finger over my chin and gave it to her straight. "You're the first woman I've ever fucked, and you want to know if I'm done with you yet," I said. "To me, that's a weird question. No. I am very much fucking not."

She bit her lip. She was unbearably beautiful, even just-fucked in the shadows of my bedroom. *Especially* then. "I think I read that in a book of poetry somewhere."

"Write it down and savor it," I said.

She put a hand on my shoulder, letting her fingers trace down my bicep. Her lashes swept down, then up again, a flicker of uncertainty I'd never seen in her before. I stared, fascinated.

"This..." She paused. "This isn't casual to me."

My throat closed. I tried to think of words, but nothing came.

"It better not be," I said at last.

For some reason, that made her exhale, like she'd been holding her breath. Had she actually been wondering? "Okay, then," she said. "This is a thing. Right? We're a thing."

I'd never seen this side of her, vulnerable and questioning. "Will you get in trouble?" I asked her.

She frowned, catching my meaning—she'd been my counselor until a few days ago, after all. "No," she said. "I don't see a reason I would. The paperwork is done. It's pretty clear we no longer have a professional relationship. And my personal relationships aren't anyone's business."

"This hasn't happened to you before? With a client?" I asked.

Her eyes went wide.

My hackles went up. "Was the last guy a client?" Silence. "The truth, Tara."

"No," she answered me. "He wasn't a client."

But there was something there, something heavy. Something she wasn't saying. *You can't be angry, dipshit,* I told myself, *because you haven't told her about the coke, have you?* The Thunderbird, the junkyard, the fire. She'd be pissed off if she knew. Disgusted, maybe. I could handle that some other day, but today was not that day.

I reached out and hooked a hand behind her knee. Pulled her gently until she had unfolded her legs and was leaning back. Then I rolled on top of her.

"No more talking," I said.

She parted her lips, looking up at me. Her hair was spread on the pillow, her dark eyes fixed on me, her mouth still rosy from kissing me.

I had Tara Montgomery naked in my bed. Suddenly, that was the only thing that mattered. I ran my thumb along her lower lip, tracing it, watching her eyes go hazy.

"We're a thing," I said simply. "No more talking."

Her voice was a whisper. "Okay, Jace."

I leaned down and kissed her. Tasted her. Those soft, beautiful lips, all mine. For now.

I kissed her, and I kissed her. And we didn't talk again.

TWENTY-ONE

Tara

BY THE END of the day on Monday, I was restless in my own skin. I had gone about my day the way I always did: seeing clients, writing emails and reports, eating lunch at my desk. If I still had sore muscles and chafed skin from Saturday night, well, I was a grownup and could ignore them. I had work to do, after all.

Except my focus kept slipping. I'd be writing an email and I'd picture the tip of Jace's cock sliding into my mouth, the way he'd said my name. I'd be sipping my afternoon cup of tea and I'd hear him say *I knew you'd fuck like this* in my ear. It was a movie that played over and over in my head, pleasant and distracting and worrisome at the same time. I wanted to see Jace, and I was terrified of seeing Jace. What was supposed to happen now?

We're a thing, Jace said in my ear. *No more talking.*

It sounded so simple. But if I could be an Olympic champion at any sport, it would be at overthinking things. This was the same office I'd been in on Friday, and I was doing the same routine. I looked the same, dressed the same, but I was a different person, and I wasn't entirely sure how.

I needed to talk to someone.

Not Jace, of course. Someone I could talk to *about* Jace. I didn't have any close female friends, something I never took the time to examine too closely. *Too busy* was my usual excuse. The girls I'd known at my private high school had all gone their separate ways as soon as we graduated, and my college acquaintances had spread around the country, going where the jobs were. Most of them were, I assumed, married by now and maybe even mothers. Which still left me no one to talk to.

My mother wasn't an option—I'd never dished to my mother about my love life, and I wasn't going to start now. I thought about Emily, the pretty blonde who was Luke Riggs' adored girlfriend, very briefly, but I couldn't quite get up the nerve to track her down. It would seem stalkery and weird.

At four-thirty, with my appointments done for the day, I walked down the hall to see Catherine Fox, one of the other counselors in the office. Catherine was in her thirties, and she was one of the best counselors we had on staff—smart, patient, straightforward, kind and authoritative at the same time. I admired her, and in lieu of friendship, that would have to do.

Her office door was open, and she saw me approach. "Tara," she said, taking off her glasses as she looked up from her computer. "Nice to see you."

I closed the door behind me. "Do you have a free counseling slot?"

"My four-thirty cancelled, so you're in luck. Do you have a referral for me?"

"Sort of," I said. "The patient is me."

Her eyebrows rose in surprise. It wasn't unheard of, of course, for counselors to need counseling—we're human, just like everyone else. But I'd never asked before. Still, Catherine took it in stride.

"Have a seat," she said.

I sat down in the chair across from her. It was crazy déjà vu, being the patient in this situation. I'd been on her side of the desk hundreds of times but never on this side at all.

"What can I help you with?" Catherine said.

I blew out a breath. If my clients could do this, then so could I. "This needs to stay confidential," I said.

"Of course."

"I'm seeing someone new."

Catherine nodded encouragingly, knowing there was more.

"He's a former client," I said. Her eyebrows rose again, so I clarified, "Our sessions were finished, and my report was written. We didn't have a professional relationship. But I saw him again, and now we have a personal one."

It reduced it to such simple terms, the relationship between Jace and me. The crazy way we'd turned each other's lives upside down.

"Still, it's unusual, to say the least," Catherine said, prodding me along. "This man must be very important to you."

I looked at her—her neat dark bob streaked with gray, her professional blouse and blazer—and then looked away, at the wall, at nothing. I was starting to understand how Jace had felt in this chair, talking about things that were secret and personal. "He is," I said. "Or he could be. I know you know the kind of clients I see, but Jace is different. He's smart, and he's..." *A con. A confidential informant. A thief. A man who reads Dostoevsky. A virgin, until I got my hands on him. Oh, and he's a natural genius at sex, and I've never come like that in my life.* "He's complex," I finished lamely. "He's interesting. Fascinating."

Catherine leaned forward in her chair and put her chin in

her hand, listening to me. It was an un-counselor-like gesture. "Tara, you're smitten," she said.

"Maybe." No, it was time for the truth. "Okay, I am."

"That's wonderful. So why are you here?"

God, this was hard. "I'm here because I'm confused," I said. "I've never crossed the line with a client, a former client, before. It feels risky. And my last relationship ended eight months ago."

"You were engaged, weren't you?" Catherine asked. Office gossip was as reliable as ever, obviously.

"We were. I broke it off. But he was a cop on the Westlake PD. And Jace just finished doing time. He knows I was engaged, but he doesn't know who I was engaged to."

Catherine still had her chin in her hand. "And you haven't told him yet."

I pressed my palms together in my lap, twisted my fingers. "This is too new. Jace won't like it—I know he won't. I don't really know how he'll react. But with the way I feel, I can't go further without telling him."

"That's a dilemma," Catherine said. "You want to hear something?"

I blinked at her. "Um, sure."

"One of my clients did a four-year stretch. She got out two years ago. She lost custody of her kids, and she hasn't gotten it back, and it depresses her. She's got a lot of problems—I won't get into it—but she's busting her ass to overcome them so she has a shot at getting her kids back. Last week she was diagnosed with ovarian cancer. Stage three."

"Oh my god," I said softly. "I'm so sorry."

"She came in here this morning and talked about what she wishes she would have done. About the time she wasted doing stupid things that made her lose her kids when she had no idea her time was so short. 'None of it was important,' she said to me, 'none of it, I know that now, and now that chance is gone.' I've worked with you for three years, Tara, and I've never seen you look like you do right now. All tied up in knots, like something actually matters."

I sat speechless.

"You're one of the most unruffled, self-contained women I've ever met," Catherine said. "Even when you were going through that breakup—and we all knew it—you didn't show a crack. Now you're asking for a therapy session and sitting in my chair, twisting your hands and worrying about this guy. And all I can think is, *Finally*. I have to assume the sex is off the charts. Is it?"

"Um..." I couldn't summon the words. "I, it was, um. It was..." I trailed off, because how should I describe what it felt like to have Jace Riggs inside of me? It was unlike anything in the world. "Yes, it is."

"I figured," Catherine said. "You've finally been banged to Heaven and back, holy angels be praised. I approve of this guy for that alone. Is he hot?"

This time, the answer slipped out easy. "So, so hot," I said.

"Ha," Catherine said. She reached over and turned her computer off. "You want my advice? Here it is. Go find your hot sex god and bang him again, and again and again until he can't stand up. Tell him about what's-his-name that no one even remembers anymore. If he tries to dump you, get him back. If he tries again, get him back again. Get him back as many times as you have to before your time is up and all you have is regrets." She picked up her purse and stood. "And next time, just ask me to go for a drink, will you? I'd rather hear the juicy details over a martini."

I drove home in a daze, and I was already in my pajamas, glass of wine in hand, before I unpacked everything she'd said. What was I doing, booking a therapy session to talk about my new boyfriend? Why hadn't I just asked Catherine if she wanted to have a drink?

Let's analyze your intimacy problem, Jace said in my head.

Damn him, was he ever wrong?

Go find your sex god and bang him until he can't stand up, before all you have is regrets.

I looked down at myself: pajama pants, loose top. I put down my glass of wine and picked up my phone. *Where are you?* I texted Jace.

Finishing work, he replied. *You?*

You know where I live, I wrote. *I'm home, and I'm naked. Your call.*

There was a second of silence. The dots on my phone moved. Stopped. Moved again.

Then the words came up: *Stay there*

The dots stopped, because he was on his way.

I smiled. Then I dropped my pants to the floor, pulled off my shirt, and stripped off my panties to make it true.

TWENTY-TWO

Jace

I NEEDED A SHOWER. I needed condoms. I needed a car.

Damn it, damn it, damn it.

I was at Riggs Auto alone when her text came in. Luke usually gave me a lift to and from work since we worked the same hours, but he'd had somewhere to go and he'd left early. Which meant I had no way to get where I was going unless I took the bus, which would take nearly an hour.

You know where I live. I'm home, and I'm naked.

When he's only had one sex session in his life—one stupendous, incredible sex session—a man's gotta do what a man's gotta do. I opened the cash drawer and took out enough money for a cab. I knew that most people took Uber these days, but credit cards are hard to get when you're a con, as are the latest phones with apps. So I used my five-year-old phone to call a taxi so I could pay the driver in cash. It wasn't stealing this time because I'd repay the money.

I had the driver take me home to the guest house, because I was hoping Luke would be home by now so I could take his Charger. But as the cab pulled away, I realized the driveway was still empty except for Emily's old Tercel. The thing only ran because Luke spent a lot of hours maintaining it—which was a sign of devotion if I ever saw one—but it did, in fact, run. If she'd lend it to me, I could get to Tara's.

First I went into the guest house, showered in record time, and changed into clean clothes. Tara had had to put up with me once without a shower, and I wasn't doing that to her again. I grabbed some of my brothers' condoms from the bathroom drawer and put them in the pocket of my leather jacket. Then I locked up and walked to the main house to work on Emily.

She answered my knock at the back door—I only ever came to the back door so that she and Luke would know it was me. She was wearing jeans and a loose flowered top, her natural blonde hair tied messily on top of her head. "You can just come in, you know," she said, giving me a smile.

I liked Emily. Her mother was one of Westlake's most prominent cops—one of the force's only female cops, a woman so good at her job that she'd moved up the ranks. It should bother me to be so closely connected to someone so high in the Westlake PD, but Nora Parker's rank meant she knew who I really was. I'd never met her, but I knew she knew, which was why she left me alone. This was the strange kind of cat-and-mouse game you play when you're a confidential informant—some cops know, some don't, and no one is allowed to talk about it either way.

Emily—and her fraternal twin sister, Lauren—had always been known as one of Westlake's good girls when we were all growing up. Beautiful, popular, good grades, the kind of girl who dated football players. At eighteen she'd stopped dating football players when she met Luke, and they dated in secret until Emily left for college. When she came back, she worked it out with Luke and now they were publicly a couple. If Emily ever took flack for being with a Riggs brother, she never let on. The way she looked at my brother made my stomach hurt with envy, but it also made her good folk in my opinion.

"We've had this conversation," I said to her. "I'm not going to just walk in. This is your house."

"It's your house, too, remember?" Emily said.

"It isn't," I replied. Really, she was never going to get me to budge on this. "Besides, I could walk in on something embarrassing."

"We've had this conversation," Emily said, shooting my words back at me. "We'd come up with a warning system if something embarrassing is going on. But Jace, you should come to the house if you want to watch TV or raid the fridge or something. Or just hang out."

I shook my head. "I'm fine in the guest house." I was. After getting out of prison, the guest house had been pretty fucking great. And Luke and I had never actually hung out—none of us Riggs brothers did that. *Try it,* a voice in the back of my mind said. *Maybe you'd like it.* But I'd have to be a different guy to do that. A guy who didn't have hangups and intimacy problems and all the other baggage I was carrying around.

"I came to ask a favor," I said.

Emily's eyebrows rose. I never asked favors, and she knew it. "What is it?"

"I need to borrow your car."

She tilted her head. "For how long?"

I scratched my chin, wondering how long I would be. Who was I kidding? "Overnight," I said.

Her eyes went wide, and immediately she started calculating. "You need to go somewhere overnight." She crossed her arms.

"And it's so important that you're willing to knock on my door and ask me a favor, which you never do."

"Yes, ma'am," I said.

"It's that brunette," Emily said, fixing her woman's laser gaze on me. "Tara Montgomery. The one who was looking for you."

I pushed my hands into my back pockets. "No comment."

"I take it she found you that night," Emily said.

"No comment," I repeated.

"Was that her car I saw parked here on the weekend?"

"Possibly."

"You like her?"

"Define 'like,'" I said.

"Does she like you?"

"You'd have to ask her that."

Emily bumped her fist lightly against the doorframe. "Damn it, Jace Riggs, you're like a brick wall. This is *important*. She was really pretty. Are you two a thing?"

I sighed. "Yes. But we won't be a thing if I don't get to go see her. Get it? Just give me a break here, Emily. Come on."

Emily groaned and sagged against the doorframe—she'd always been the dramatic type. "Jace, I don't know how you do it, but you're adorable. *Adorable*." She disappeared into the house and came back with a key ring, which she tossed at me. "Take it," she said. "It needs a good crank to start. If it idles too long, it sometimes dies. And the wipers are fussy, you have to flick them like five times."

"Thanks," I said, meaning it.

"I want to meet her. Again. And I'm telling Luke."

Jesus. So much for privacy. Well, I was willing to sacrifice it.

I gave her a salute and left the back porch, headed for the driveway. I didn't need directions. For the first time in my life, I knew exactly where I was going.

TWENTY-THREE

Tara

THIS WAS HARDER than it seemed at first. I'd felt bold when I sent that text, but the longer Jace took to get here, the less bold I got. I sipped my wine until my glass was empty, then thought maybe I shouldn't have another. I thought about putting makeup on, then decided that would be too much. I thought about taking a shower, but my hair would be wet when he got here. I thought about eating something—even though I was too nervous to be hungry—but what if that made my belly pop out? There was no way to hide it. I was naked, after all.

Naked. Right, I was naked. I had to remember that and not think too much about it at the same time. Because if I thought too much about it, the usual female doubts would creep in. I hadn't been working out as much as I should be since the breakup—I'd been too busy, too preoccupied, and with no one to see me, it seemed like it didn't matter. I didn't have a Brazilian wax or a bikini wax or any other kind of wax—for the same reasons as the lack of working out. And then there were my small boobs, which I'd been painfully self-conscious of until I'd learned better. My boobs were given to me by God and genetics, there was nothing I could do about them, and anyone who didn't like them knew where they could put their opinion.

Except... Jace would see they were small. It was so obvious, standing here naked. *Jace has already seen them, you idiot,* I told myself firmly. *You didn't hear him complain.*

I stared at my empty wine glass and wished he'd hurry up.

Let's talk about your intimacy problem. Well, I was doing something about it, wasn't I? I just wished it wasn't so freaking terrifying.

My phone rang, making me jump. I grabbed it off the counter. It was Jace. *Oh shit, he's standing me up.*

"Hey," I said, trying to sound casual when I answered.

"Tara," he said, and the tone of his low voice made my spine jump. "I'm downstairs. I know your building, but I don't know what apartment you're in."

I ran a hand through my hair. He was right, of course—I'd never told him. He'd dropped me off in front of my building, but he hadn't come in. We were both bad at this booty-call thing. "Third floor," I said. "Apartment 302."

"You still naked?" he asked.

My heart did a loud thump in my chest. "Yes, Jace."

"Unlock the door," he said and hung up.

I buzzed him in, put the phone down, and turned the bolt lock on my door. Then, in a last-minute attack of nerves, I turned out the overhead lights and turned a lamp on instead. I had just stood straight again when the door clicked open and closed again.

I turned. Jace was in my apartment, all six feet plus of him, jeans on his long legs, a black tee, his black leather jacket. He had stopped at the door, his ocean-gray gaze moving over me, taking me in.

"Jesus," he said softly.

I stood to face him. I brushed my long hair back behind my shoulders so he could see. I could feel my nipples going hard.

His eyes went dark and a muscle twitched in his jaw, but he didn't move. He kept looking at me—not just my breasts, not just between my legs, but all of me. Finally, his gaze moved back up to my face and he caught my eyes. The darkness was still there, but it was softened by something more thoughtful. He had the most fascinatingly expressive face I'd ever seen. I could stare at Jace Riggs forever.

The silence stretched out. It should have felt awkward and uncomfortable, but somehow it didn't. It felt warm, like we were talking without talking. Finally, Jace turned and locked my door behind him in one graceful turn of his wrist. Then he turned and came toward me.

He didn't rush. He didn't swagger. He just crossed the room until he stood in front of me, and then he put his hands on my waist. His touch was warm and hard, smoothing over my skin until he had pulled me toward him, his palms on my spine. I let myself press into him as he ran his hands slowly, gently up and down my back.

I could feel everything against my naked skin—the cold teeth of the zipper on his jacket, the cool hardness of the leather, even the press of his belt buckle against my belly. My nipples brushed against him, hard and vulnerable. My bare thighs brushed his jeans. I could smell leather and soap—he'd had a shower—and the scent of Jace's skin. It was a smell I'd reimagined a dozen times since the last time I'd seen him.

I put my hands on his chest beneath his jacket and smoothed them upward. This wasn't how I'd imagined this would go—I'd pictured something wild, more animalistic. He hadn't even grabbed my ass or touched my nipples. But I stood there with his hands on my back and his hard, warm chest beneath my palms, and something inside me cracked open instead. I felt like I'd never been naked with a man before. I'd never been *this* naked with a man before, and it almost made me feel like weeping.

Before I could do anything stupid, like sob, Jace's big hand moved to the back of my head, tangling through my long hair, and he lowered his head and kissed me. A long, sweet, open kiss that made everything inside me come alive. We'd never done this yet—just stood face to face and kissed. The next thing I knew I was up on my toes, my arms around his neck, my hands in his soft hair as he wrapped his big arms tightly around me. He pressed my whole body against him, nearly lifting me off my feet. His beard rasped against my skin and our tongues tangled like we were teenagers. Beneath the cool of the leather jacket he was warm, so warm. His clothes pressing against my bare skin was exciting and frustrating at the same time.

He broke the kiss and dropped his mouth to my neck. One of his hands brushed over my hair, smoothing the strands, and I could feel my pulse in my throat. My fingers tightened on the back of his neck.

"Jace," I managed to say, "I'm naked."

His mouth was traveling slowly over the side of my neck, savoring it. His hand moved down and finally slid over the soft flesh of my ass, exploring the curve of it, then cupping it gently. "You are beautifully naked," he said softly in my ear.

I couldn't breathe for a long moment. Then I remembered what I was going to say. "You have clothes on," I said. "Take them off."

"I'd rather look at you," he rumbled against my neck.

"I wouldn't," I said. God, did I know his hair was soft before?

I couldn't remember. "I've been standing here for a while. I've seen enough of me."

His answer was immediate. "There's no such thing as seeing enough of you."

I couldn't breathe again. Then I brushed my fingertips over his trim beard. "I'd rather see you."

He grumbled again, but I pushed at the leather jacket and he allowed it to drop to the floor. He took his arms off me just long enough for it to be gone, and then he put them around me again. It wasn't enough, but at least I had access to his arms now, bare beneath his tee. I ran my hands over his forearms, the insides of his elbows, his biceps, exploring them as he bent and kissed me again.

He bent his knees and lifted me, and my legs wrapped around him of their own accord, gripping his hips like we did this every day. He didn't take his mouth from mine but walked us into my kitchen like I weighed nothing. I broke the kiss and gasped as I felt the cold of the counter beneath my ass.

He let go of my waist and his hands moved up to my breasts, engulfing them easily, his thumbs brushing over my nipples. He bent his knees again and lowered down to put his mouth on my nipple as I moaned and dug my hands into his hair.

"More clothes off," I gasped.

"You're impatient," he said, moving to the other nipple.

I was. I yanked at his shirt from my awkward angle, and he gave in and pulled it off, tossing it away. He returned to my nipples and I gasped again as the sensation shot through me, down my belly and between my legs. I needed him there. I needed him *there*.

But I didn't want to do it on the kitchen counter. My plan for wild, animalistic sex had disappeared. I didn't want to do it that way, not with this man, not in this moment. "The bed," I told him, my voice choked.

He understood, like he always did. He straightened, his hands smoothing down the small of my back. He lifted me again like a feather, and the next thing I knew I was on my back on the bed with Jace over me.

We'd done this before in his guest house—me on the bed, Jace braced over me, his big arms flexed. That had been dirty and raw and spectacular, a first time for the record books. This time I pulled him down to me and kissed him while his hands moved down my sides, over my belly, making me shiver. His hand slid back up over my breast and he bit my lip gently as his thumb brushed over my throat. He hadn't even touched me between my legs yet and I was going crazy.

I undid his belt, the buttons on his jeans, and slid my hand inside, rubbing him. He braced himself over me on one hand and with the other he pinned my free hand to the mattress. He looked down at me, his dark mussed hair falling forward, his gray eyes never leaving mine.

"Christ, you're gorgeous," he said.

Happiness bubbled up through me. I'd never in my life had a man look at me the way this one did. I hadn't been made with curves that men stared at, the kind that drove them wild, but Jace looked at me like he'd never seen a sexier woman in his life. I felt voluptuous and female and perfect. "No talking," I said, letting my hand travel over him, feeling his heat and his length.

The corner of his mouth quirked, though he was fighting to keep control. "The condoms are in my jacket. In the other room."

"We don't need them." I'd been thinking about this while standing naked in my apartment, waiting for him to come. "I'm on the pill. I know you're clean. And I am, too. I got tested after..." I couldn't say more. Kyle had no place in this bed. "After," I finished lamely.

His look was shocked and turned on at the same time. "Are you fucking serious?"

I leaned up and brushed my mouth over his lower lip. "I am fucking serious," I told him.

His body had gone hard, his shoulders and arms tense. He was processing the idea, letting it sink in. I had to remember this was only the second time for him, that maybe it was too much too soon. Maybe I was pushing him. Maybe he wouldn't be comfortable. Maybe—

Then he was off the bed, and I heard the last of his clothes hit the floor. The bed sagged as he got on again, fully naked, miles and miles of sleek hot muscle. The dark dusting of hair on his flat belly fascinated me, his lean hips, his strong thighs. And his cock, powerful and vulnerable. He knelt between my legs, pushed them apart. He lowered his head and trailed his mouth over my belly as his fingers finally slid into my pussy.

I moaned in pleasure, pushing my hips up off the bed. He stroked me, his clever fingertips finding me everywhere, every slick crevice that was waiting for him. "What do you want, Tara?" he asked, his breath against the skin of my belly.

"You," I said.

Jace's teeth scraped me for a second as he thought about that. "That's a good answer." He moved up over me, kissed my mouth, and pushed the tip of his cock inside me, bare.

It was like lightning. We both gasped. Jace dropped his mouth to my neck and pushed in further, further. "Fuck, that's good," he said.

I reached down and gripped his perfect ass, pulling him into me. I felt wild, happy and at the same time terrified that this would end. "Why is it so good with you?" I said into the skin of his shoulder. "It isn't like anything else. It's incredible. I don't know why."

"Because of you," he said, pushing all the way in until he filled me. I could feel his bare skin, his pulse inside me. And then, instead of fucking me, he drew out again and rubbed his fingers where he'd just been.

"Jace," I said. "*Jesus.*"

"I like to watch you come," he said.

He was going to see it. I was climbing toward orgasm, but I wanted him to fuck me. "I need you," I said, nearly begging. "I need you."

His hand left me and he pushed his cock inside me again, a long slow pump as I gripped him and moaned. "God, where did you *learn* this?" I said as he withdrew from me again and I tried not to whimper. "I thought inexperienced guys were supposed to be fast."

He laughed quietly against the side of my neck as his fingers found me *again.* "When you wait this long, you learn restraint," he said, his thumb slowly circling my clit. "It's been so many years, I can wait a few more minutes."

"Oh," I said. I was rising, rising. "Don't you want—"

His teeth scraped my skin, his beard dragging over it. "Don't mistake me, Tara," he said. "I very much want. I want my come inside you. I want it in your mouth, on your skin. I want it in your ass. I want it everywhere, because I want everything."

"Yes," I said. "Yes."

"I'm going to have it," he said.

I couldn't wait. "Yes," I said again.

He pressed my clit with the pad of his thumb and I came, arching and crying out. Jace put a hand on my hip and thrust inside me so I was squeezing him as I kept coming. Then he gave me what I wanted and fucked me, fast and hard and slick, his cock perfect inside me, making the aftershocks of the orgasm pound through me, drawing them out over and over. I was delirious and sore and it felt better than anything. He gripped the back of my knee and came with a groan, his come releasing inside me long and hard.

He dropped his face to my neck as we both fought for breath. His hand came up and his thumb drew over my cheekbone once, a slow caress. He ran the backs of his fingers over my jaw, my throat, and then gently touched my hair, his fingertips moving through the tousled strands.

My throat closed as I stared at the ceiling, breathing him in. This wasn't sex. Well, it was—it *was*—but at the same time it wasn't. There were no words for what this was. There were no words for how it filled me with happiness and terrified me at the same time. There were no words for Jace Riggs and his gray eyes and his hands on my skin and the way he felt inside me, no words for the woman I was with him, a woman who was whole and full and powerful and vulnerable for the first time in her life.

He rolled off me, withdrawing from me, and lay on his back on the pillow next to me. I turned my head and watched him slowly scrape his hands over his face. I was mesmerized yet again by his hands, his fingers with their understated rings, the way his beard made a rasping sound against his palms, the way he pressed his fingertips briefly into the skin of his forehead and his temples, massaging it. "Jesus Christ," he said softly.

I rolled over onto one side so I could watch him more openly. "Talk to me," I said, because with me it was words, always words.

Jace laughed, dropping his hands, and once again he was oblivious to how I froze in fascination and awe. "Tara, I can't say a fucking thing."

He'd had plenty to say a few minutes ago, every word of it burned into my brain. Even now, with my body humming with satisfied contentment, I was willing to let him do all of those things. I could feel the warm trickle of him between my legs, but I didn't want to get up yet.

"Luke knows about us," Jace said. "Or he will, as soon as he gets home and Emily tells him."

"Emily knows?"

"I had to borrow her car to come over here."

Shit. I should have thought about that when I'd texted him. "I thought there was a car you were working on," I said. "It isn't ready yet?"

He stared at the ceiling for a moment, his gray eyes unreadable. "It had problems," he said. "I had to get rid of it. I'll get another one."

I put my palm to his warm shoulder and rested my chin on the back of my hand. "I'm sorry. I didn't think."

He glanced at me. "Don't ever say sorry for getting naked and inviting me over." He looked at the ceiling again. "Anyway, I borrowed Emily's car, and she figured everything out. Which means Luke knows, and eventually my other brothers will, too."

"Does that bother you?" I asked him.

"No," he replied honestly.

"I'd like to meet them."

That made him hesitate. "My brothers are difficult people," he said. "We all thought Ryan would have a big baseball career, but that's over, I think for good. Dex flunked off the police force, and there were rumors he was corrupt. We've fucked up a lot of things in our lives. We aren't really upstanding guys, the kind of guys you want to get to know."

"Jace," I said, "I see screwed-up people for a living. Your brothers don't scare me. Besides, you wish you were closer to them. I can tell by the way you talk about them."

His brows drew down as he thought this over. "We've never been close," he said, hedging. Then he added, "The truth is, I didn't think that was an option."

I drew my fingertip along his bearded jaw. "It's an option," I said. "Why wouldn't it be?"

He thought about it some more, then glanced at me, a wry spark of amusement in his eyes. "Thank you, counselor," he said.

I leaned over and brushed my lips over his. "You're welcome."

I kissed him again, and there it was, that spark that never went out.

This man. This man.

"Session's over," I told Jace Riggs. "What else are we going to do?"

TWENTY-FOUR

Jace

I GOT DRESSED and left at six o'clock in the morning. It was a weekday, and Tara had to go to work. For that matter, so did I.

It wasn't easy to leave. Jesus, how many times had we had sex last night? Three? That wasn't even counting the blow job she'd given me when we'd finally come up for air long enough to take a shower. The memory of Tara Montgomery's mouth on my cock was going down as one of the best things that had ever happened to me, bar none. I'd be reliving it when I was ninety, how she'd pushed her wet hair back and gone down on her knees. It was one of those things that made a man wonder what the hell he'd done to deserve it.

Still, I put on my jeans and my tee, my boots and my leather jacket. I'd said a sleepy goodbye to Tara after a few hours' sleep, because taking off while she was sleeping was not how I roll. I kissed her and told her I'd talk to her later.

I didn't tell her I loved her, that she was the only thing that fucking mattered to me, because after so long alone, that shit is hard. But I was kind of hoping she was getting the idea.

Emily's car took a hard crank to start, as advertised. I felt like a giant inside this tiny Tercel, but even so, it felt good to be driving again. I'd told Tara that cars were in my blood, and I meant it. When I was driving I didn't feel like a con or a failure or a guy who'd waited until twenty-five to get laid. I just felt like Jace Riggs. The only thing better was the way I felt when I was with Tara.

There was no traffic in Westlake at this hour, with dawn still slowly lighting the sky and the street lights still switching off. I felt like I had the town to myself. I was relaxed and bone-tired and I felt so different that I was almost outside myself. I was lost in thought when the cherry lights started flashing in my rearview mirror, telling me a cop was pulling me over.

It made no sense. I wasn't speeding and I hadn't missed a light or a sign. Maybe the taillights on Emily's car were out, or there was a problem with her license plate, but deep down I didn't think so. I had a feeling that something was about to go very fucking bad.

I pulled over, rolled my window down, and waited for the cop. He took his time, parking behind me and leaving his lights on, strolling slowly up as I watched him in my rearview mirror. He was alone, a fit guy with light brown hair and a uniform that fit like a glove.

"License and registration," he said when he got to my window.

I handed him my license, then flipped open the glove box and rifled through it. Damn it, there was no registration in here. I looked again.

"Registration," the cop said, harder this time.

So it was going to be this way. Fine. "It isn't here," I said to him.

The cop shifted his weight. "Is this your car?"

"No. I borrowed it."

"You borrowed it."

"Yes."

There was a long pause. "Step out of the car, Mr. Riggs."

I did as I was told. The cop was a few inches shorter than me, and when he looked me up and down I caught a hot blast of disgust and resentment. I tried to think of what I'd done to piss him off and could think of nothing.

"Where are you coming from?" the cop asked me.

"My girlfriend's place," I said.

The cop's eyes went hard as flint as he looked at me. "Is that fucking so?"

Something ticked over in my mind. An idea, maybe. This wasn't just a traffic stop. It was personal somehow. But how?

The cop held up my driver's license between two fingers, then flicked it into the dirt at the side of the road. "You're a convicted felon, Mr. Riggs," he said, "and you're driving a car that isn't yours. That gives me the right to search your vehicle."

He hadn't run my license, yet he knew I had a record. He hadn't run my plates either. What he was saying about his rights was probably bullshit. Still, I said, "Go ahead."

He put me against the car and patted me down first. His hand in my jacket pocket found the condoms I'd put there, and he pulled them out.

"I told you," I said. "I was at my girlfriend's."

The cop dropped the condoms into the dirt next to my driver's license. "Unfuckingbelievable," he said, the word spitting with contempt. "As if she'd give you the time of day."

I went still. Every alarm in my body was wide awake and screaming. *Think, Jace, think.* Who the fuck was this guy? If he knew who I was, he'd been looking for me. Targeting me. Which meant he'd followed me—from Tara's.

He'd staked me out at Tara's.

And then I figured it out.

I remembered Tara sitting across from me in the Greek restaurant, her cheeks flushed after she'd had a few glasses of wine. *I don't know what to tell you about Kyle,* she'd said.

Tara's face when I'd asked if the man she almost married was a client. *No,* she'd said, *not a client,* but there had been something she wasn't saying. Something big. Something fucking huge, and I was so wrapped up in her, so worried that this thing would die before it started, that I hadn't asked her.

He was nice, she'd said. *I only sort of loved him. The sex was terrible.* I watched the cop open the back passenger door and stare into the car's empty back seat, a frown on his good-looking face, and I knew. I knew the way an alpha dog knows that another alpha dog is on his territory. Tara's ex was a cop. A fucking cop. And he knew about me.

The cop slammed the passenger door and straightened, looking at me over the roof of the car. "Keep your hands on the car," he said, though I hadn't moved.

I just stared back at him and said nothing.

He narrowed his eyes at me. "You have something to say, Riggs?"

"You think this is going to get her back?" I asked him.

"Fuck you," he spat, and I knew I was right.

Tara's ex-boyfriend, the man she almost married, was a cop. And she'd never told me.

He rounded to the back of the car and opened the trunk. He stared into it, pushing things around—if I knew anything about Luke, he'd put a jack and a jump kit in Emily's car at the very least. I watched as Kyle the cop yanked up the panel where the spare tire was kept, stared into the well blankly for a second, then pushed the panel down again.

My blood was pounding in my ears. I stood rigid, unmoving. He'd looked in the fucking wheel well. Where the coke was stashed in my last car.

Because he was looking for it.

And now he seemed pissed because it wasn't there. He slammed the trunk and looked at me, his face going red. "Whose fucking car is this?" he asked.

I made my voice stay even. "A friend's."

"Is it?" The cop came around the car, coming closer to me. "Or is it yours?"

"It's a friend's."

"Fuck you, liar."

I couldn't help it. "I borrowed the car," I told him, "but your ex-girlfriend is mine."

I was half expecting the hit. He caught me under the jaw with his fist while kicking the back of my knees at the same time. I tried to brace myself, but I still lost my balance and dropped to my knees. My arm came up just as his cop's boot took a swing at my face, and I blocked it.

"You fucking piece of shit," Kyle said. He drew his boot back and took another hit, this time to my kidneys. Pain flashed up my back and down into my stomach, and I tried not to fall over. He took another kick and connected with my temple and my world went white for a second before I found myself on my back in the dirt.

I blinked my eyes open to see him standing over me, looking down. "A Riggs," he said. "A fucking *Riggs*, of all people. I thought Tara would stoop low, but I didn't think she'd stoop that low." He leaned closer. "Tell me where you put it, and maybe I'll get you and your brothers off the hook and out of federal prison."

The coke. He was talking about the coke. My head was throbbing, as was my spine, but I kept my eyes open and held his gaze. "I don't know what you're talking about," I said.

"Everyone says you're the smart one, but you're not that fucking smart. All it took was a little bit of money to one of your employees, and you had a present left in your car. No one is loyal to you, Riggs. No one is loyal to any of you. Your entire family is Westlake's embarrassment. Your father, your brothers, and you. If you think you're protected because Luke Riggs is fucking Nora Parker's daughter, you're wrong. She might not have the guts to get rid of you, but the rest of us on the force do."

I breathed through my closed throat and said nothing.

He kept talking. "Maybe you hid the shit, but there's a raid coming down at Riggs Auto. They're busting the door down right now. Wherever you hid it, we'll find it. And you and your brothers will go down."

Jesus. This was bigger than I'd imagined, than any of us had imagined. The only card I had in my pocket was that Officer Kyle obviously didn't know about the fire at Casey's junkyard—or he hadn't connected the dots yet. But he would. I had no doubt he would. Sweat broke out on the back of my neck.

Why? I wanted to ask him. *Why?* But I already knew the answer to that, didn't I? He'd told me so himself.

I was a Riggs. I was born one, and I'd always be one. It was a life sentence.

"As for Tara," Officer Kyle said, "the fact that you put your fucking hands on her disgusts me. I wanted to get her back, but now she's damaged goods. I wouldn't touch her if she begged me. Still, though, here's a little souvenir from me to you."

The blow from his boot hit me hard right over the eye. I felt the skin scrape off on his sole as the pain pounded through my skull. My world wavered again but the lights didn't go out.

He was trying to provoke me. Deep down, I knew that—that he wanted me to get up, to charge him. Even better, to pull a weapon. I was a con who had just finished parole, and assaulting a police officer would be just the ticket for him to put me away—or shoot me—with no questions asked.

He wanted me to do it. He was *dying* for me to do it. I looked in his face, and I knew that was true. He wanted me to make a move. And I wanted to do it more than I've wanted to do almost anything in my life. In that moment, my rage was so white-hot I could have put my hands around his neck and squeezed.

I could do it. I could kill him right fucking now. This man who had me in the dirt after all I'd done, after I'd tried so hard. This man who could kick me on the ground because he knew I was dead if I got up.

"I bet you think you're protected, don't you?" the cop said as he stared down at me. "Because you're a CI. I bet you think I can't touch you." Surprise must have shown in my eyes, because he grinned. "I bet you think no one can touch you, but you're wrong. I know who you are. I also know you pissed off some very dangerous people. All I have to do is make a phone call, and the hit is out and your life is over. We were happy enough to watch you and your brothers swing for the coke, but now you've fucked my girlfriend. You think I won't make that call?"

I stayed on the ground and looked up at him and said nothing.

Officer Kyle and I stared each other down for a long minute, alpha to alpha.

"I will end you," I said to him, my voice low. A promise.

He grinned again. "No," he said. "I don't think you will."

Still I stayed on the ground as he walked away. As he got in his cruiser and drove off.

Only when the sound of his motor vanished in the distance and I was alone on the road did I sit up. I picked up my driver's license, but I left my condoms in the roadside dirt. I got up gingerly and brushed myself off, feeling myself sway with dizziness from the head blows.

Think, Riggs. Think.

This isn't over. It's never over. Not until you're dead. So what's next?

I got in Emily's car and started it while warm blood ran down the side of my face. I pulled out onto the highway and drove, not knowing where I was going, not thinking. My thoughts were spinning.

I couldn't go home, or to Riggs Auto. I had a little bit of money, and Officer Kyle hadn't taken my phone. Other than that, I had the clothes on my back and that was it.

I mopped some of the blood out of my eye with my jacket cuff and kept driving. I didn't think the drug bust was a lie—I had to warn my brothers, especially Luke. When it came out that the Thunderbird had burned in a fire in Casey's dump, my brothers would get questioned. We'd done it clean, but I hoped to God we hadn't made any mistakes. There were no drugs in the shop, and no evidence we'd set that fire, so in the end we'd probably skate on that one.

The bigger problem was what Officer Kyle had said about me being an informant. He knew who I was, which meant he was telling the truth about knowing the enemies I'd made. He'd pulled me over coming from a night at his ex-girlfriend's house with my pockets full of condoms—he was fucking furious. I had no doubt he'd make good on his threat and make that call.

When he made that call, my life was forfeit, and so were my brothers' if I avoided the hit.

If I disappeared, drove myself south and over the border to Tijuana or north and over the border to Canada, my enemies would kill my brothers in retaliation. And probably Tara.

I couldn't run. I couldn't dodge this. I'd made my choices years ago, and now I had to face the consequences.

I drove and drove, and slowly, through the haze of pain and anger, I felt a plan start to form. Something I just might be able to do.

It would be a sacrifice, but it would be worth it.

I pulled over, took out my phone, and made some calls. I sent a text.

Then I started the car, got back on the road, and went in the other direction, heading for the freeway to Detroit.

TWENTY-FIVE

Tara

I WAS AT WORK, writing emails at my desk, when my phone rang. I was on my third cup of coffee, pulling through the day and trying to stay awake after the wild experience that was last night.

I wasn't just sore; my blood was humming, my skin warm. I had picked up my phone a dozen times to text Jace, but each time I'd put it down again. I was twenty-seven, and a professional at work. As tempting as it was, I didn't want to be that woman.

Still, it was closing in on lunch time. There wasn't a rule about texting your boyfriend on your lunch hour.

My boyfriend. I had a tall, tatted, ex-con boyfriend, and I was pretty damned happy about it. I was so happy that I was already wondering if I could see him tonight. Maybe I'd come to the guest house. Jace had years of sexual experience to make up for, after all, and there were lots of things we still hadn't tried. We could—

My phone rang. It wasn't my desk phone, but my personal

cell phone, sitting in my desk drawer. I'd put it on silent, but I could hear it buzzing and buzzing. I should probably ignore it like the professional I was, but I cracked and pulled the drawer open, taking out the phone in case it was Jace.

It wasn't Jace. I didn't recognize the number. I thought of not answering, but there was a chime of unease deep in my stomach. I gave this cell number out to no one—literally no one. My parents had it, and Kyle, and John my boss in case he needed to reach me after hours. And now Jace. Frowning, I swiped the phone and answered it. "Hello?"

"Tara," came the low voice on the other end of the line, unfamiliar yet familiar at the same time. "It's Luke Riggs."

Luke Riggs had my number? There was only one person who could have given it to him. Which meant something was wrong. I felt my stomach twist. "Luke? What is it?"

"Where the hell did he go?" Luke said.

"What?"

"Jace. Where the hell did he go?"

I stared blankly at my desk. "I don't know what you're talking about."

"He went to see you last night," Luke said, his voice tight like he was trying not to shout. "He didn't come home this morning. He didn't come to the shop. I have no idea where the fuck he is."

I pushed my chair back. "That makes no sense. He left my place early. Like six."

"Have you talked to him since?"

"No."

"Neither have I. I got a text from him giving me this number and telling me to watch out for you and make sure you're okay. He won't answer his phone, his texts, anything. So where the fuck did he go?"

"I don't know." Jace wanted Luke to make sure I was okay? Why? I stood up, though there was nowhere I could go, nothing I could think of to do. "When he left this morning, he said he was going home to go to work." Oh, god. If Jace didn't make it home, then something must have happened. "Did you try calling the hospital? Maybe he got in an accident?"

"I haven't had time to do a lot of phone calls," Luke said, "because first thing this morning I had a team of cops at the door to the shop with a search warrant. They searched Riggs Auto and questioned me for hours on some bullshit charge. They just left twenty minutes ago. Jace warned me about that, too. Before he dropped off the face of the planet, he warned me that the cops were coming. He knew. So think again, and tell me—where did Jace get that information? And where did he go?"

I couldn't put it together at first. Jace had left me to go home —I knew he wasn't lying about that. But somewhere on his way home, something had happened. He'd texted Luke to tell him to call me, and he'd texted about the cops—the cops—

My knees went rubbery with shock. Kyle. It couldn't be, and yet somehow I knew it was.

"Tara?" Luke said.

"Where are you now?" I asked him. "Are you home? I'll come over."

"Just tell me where he is," Luke said, and then there was a voice in the background and the phone changed hands.

"Tara?" A woman's voice. Emily.

"I don't know where Jace is," I told her. "Let me make a phone call and I'll come over."

"He's not at the hospital," Emily said. "I tried that. I lent him my car last night, and twenty minutes ago I got a text from him. He says he's sorry, but he's not bringing my car back right now. That means he went somewhere, right? Luke has just spent hours being questioned, and I'm losing my mind."

"I'll be right there," I said. "Just let me make a phone call."

There was a second of silence. "Tara, what aren't you telling us? We need to know."

"I'll tell you everything when I get there. Just give me a few minutes. I'll see you as soon as I can." I hung up and hit the dial button on a different number, jabbing it with my thumb.

Kyle picked up on the second ring. "Yeah?"

He sounded cocky and angry and full of himself, and suddenly the anger rose in my throat, threatening to choke me. "What did you do?" I said. "Kyle, what the hell did you do?"

He was quiet for a second, probably deciding whether to play dumb. His anger won out. "A Riggs, Tara?" he said. "Was he one of your fucking charity cases? And to think I was worried about you fucking someone on the force."

"My life is none of your business," I said. "None. You move on to your dating sites and your cop bunnies, and I'll move on to whoever I want."

"You think he's a great guy?" Kyle said. "Did he tell you about the six kilos of coke in his car?"

I was struck silent. But that made no sense. "You're lying," I said.

"I am not fucking lying, you stupid bitch. Your ex-con boyfriend had six kilos of coke stashed in the trunk of his car. We raided Riggs Auto this morning."

"No," I said, but now I was remembering what Jace had said to me last night when I'd asked about his car. *It had problems. I had to get rid of it. I'll get another one.* "No."

"You want to see the search warrant?" Kyle said.

But I'd just talked to Luke, who was released and home with Emily. There was no way he'd be home if they'd found drugs at Riggs Auto. "You looked for six kilos of coke, but you didn't find them, did you? They weren't there."

"That's because he got rid of them," Kyle said. "We have a report from a dirtbag on the outskirts of town that someone set fire to the back of his dump lot. What do you want to bet that was your precious boyfriend and his brothers, burning evidence?"

"You are so full of *shit*," I said, angry again. "Jace is not a drug dealer."

"Right, he's just a car thief," Kyle said sarcastically. "That's so much better. He's an ex-con, and his father is in prison for dealing in stolen cars and a bunch of other shit. His brothers are scum who are no better than he is, and one of them is a corrupt cop. You're telling me Jace Riggs didn't do a little dealing to make money after he got out of jail? A guy like him? You're dreaming, Tara. I cannot fucking believe you."

I closed my eyes. Kyle didn't know Jace. No one knew Jace—no one except his brothers and me. This was what I was up against, being with Jace: everyone making assumptions, thinking they know what they don't know. This was what it was going to be like all the time.

That was, if I ever saw Jace again.

Jace, where did you go? Were you afraid of getting arrested? Where did you go?

Of course he was afraid of getting arrested—of course he was. A cocaine charge was enough to put him away forever. "So what did you do?" I said to Kyle. "You got to him somehow?"

"Not somehow," Kyle said. "He was right there, front and center. We've been keeping an eye on him and his brothers. I got on shift this morning and got a call from one of the guys on the overnight. Jace had gone to an address last night and never left. Turned out it was yours."

My stomach sank. "So you stepped in, and let me guess. You pulled him over."

"Like taking candy from a baby," Kyle said. "I was mad, but maybe Riggs was disappointed. You're a lousy fuck. Were you a cold fish with him, Tara, like you were with me?"

I swallowed my fury. I wanted to shout at him, but of course that was what Kyle wanted. That was always what Kyle wanted. "You don't understand anything," I said through clenched teeth. "Not about Jace, not about me, not about anything."

"If you mean I don't know that your ex-con cock is a CI, too late," Kyle said. "I know that, too. And I don't care."

Jesus, could this get any worse? Jace's whole world was blown apart, and I'd been sitting here at my desk, oblivious. "Just tell me one thing," I said. "Why? Why Jace? Why the Riggs family? What did they ever do to you?"

"It wasn't personal, Tara," Kyle said. "It was just a little housecleaning. Even with Mike Riggs put away, the Riggs brothers are a dirty stain in the middle of Westlake. It's easier if they just go. So we arranged some encouragement. But this morning, when Jace Riggs left your place..." He paused, and I knew his good ol' boy tone was a lie. Kyle was furiously angry. "It got very fucking personal this morning. Your new boyfriend is dead. I hope he was worth it."

And with that, he hung up.

TWENTY-SIX

Jace

IT WAS one o'clock in the afternoon, but my brother Dex was just getting out of bed. I knew this because I was sitting in his apartment, watching him put on a disintegrating pair of jeans. "You want a coffee?" he said to me.

"No," I said.

"Well, fuck that," Dex said. "I was going to send you out to get me one." He buttoned the jeans and looked at me. "Jesus, your face looks terrible."

I dropped into a chair. I had never been to Dex's place before. He lived in a crappy rental apartment in a faceless Detroit high rise with scratched floors and dents in the walls. The furniture was what should be called *hopeless bachelor chic* since it wouldn't have looked out of place in my guest house. "I'll explain," I said.

Dex sat on the sofa across from me and rummaged through the junk that littered the coffee table. He hadn't bothered to put on a shirt. He wasn't as hard-muscled as I was, but we had close to the same build—strong, not bulky. Dex had a tat on one bicep—he'd gone easy on the ink, like Ryan, because he'd been a cop. Other than that, his physique was lean and mean. Growing up, Dex had always been the master of the dirty fight. He probably still was.

He found what he was looking for, which was a small bowl with weed in it. "Helps me think," he said as he dug out his rolling papers.

My head was throbbing and my temple hurt. I could feel that the blood had dried on my cheek and my jaw. I should probably get up and wash it off, but I didn't want to move. I was suddenly very fucking tired.

I opened my mouth to talk when a voice came from the bedroom behind us. "God, what *time* is it?" A woman. "Fuck me, I have to go to work!"

"Then go," Dex said without looking up from his papers.

There was a minute of shuffling, and then a woman came out of the bedroom. Even half asleep and disheveled, she was ridiculously sexy—long legs, a fall of honey-blonde hair, dark-lashed eyes, pouty lips. She wore black leggings and an oversized camisole over a black lace bra. "Where are my shoes?" she mused aloud, and then she saw me, dried blood and all. "Oh, hi."

"Hi," I said politely.

"This is my brother," Dex said to the woman, barely glancing at her. "Now go."

The woman rolled her eyes. "You're an asshole." The words had no sting to them. She poked around the apartment, found a pair of three-inch heels in the corner, and put them on. She walked over to Dex—how women balanced on those things, I would never know—and slid a hand over his bare shoulder. "Bye, sexy."

Dex flinched. "Go," he said again. It was his usual I-don't-give-a-fuck tone, but I knew better. I'd seen that flinch, and I saw the brief look in his eyes when she touched him. I recognized it. It was pure, unadulterated misery, and for a split second it overtook Dex like he was going to throw up.

The woman didn't notice. She gave a huff and a giggle and walked out the door.

"You don't even like her," I observed to my brother.

Dex glanced up at me from where he was rolling his joint. "She called me last night," he said. "She was looking for a fuck. I was supposed to say no?"

That was Dex's usual MO: let women come to him. I heard Tara's voice in my head. *That's how people express, however unsatisfyingly, their desire to be close to another person, even for a short time.* She was so fucking smart. "You should find a nice girl," I said to Dex. "Someone who's good for you."

Dex licked his rolling paper. "So should you."

"I did, but it's all fucked up. I think I'm going to lose her."

Dex lowered his unlit joint and made the sign of the cross with the side of his hand, like the Pope. "Bless you, my son, for you are truly a Riggs," he said. "Now tell me what's going on."

So there had been a nice woman that Dex had screwed it up with. I briefly wondered who she was. It was interesting, but it wasn't the reason I was here. My phone started to buzz, and I knew that someone—probably Luke—had told Tara that I was gone. I quickly powered my phone off before I could read her texts and put the phone back in my pocket. "The coke was a setup," I said to Dex.

Dex had his lighter in his hand, but he went still. "What?"

"Straight up," I said. "A setup courtesy of the Westlake PD."

Dex's dark blue eyes narrowed as he thought it through. "Nora Parker?"

"Not her," I said about Emily's mother. "The rest of them. They think she's gone soft on us because of Luke and Emily."

"So plant some coke at Riggs Auto, and we're done," Dex said. "Shit, I should have seen it."

"There was a raid on the garage this morning," I said. "I warned Luke it was coming."

Dex found his phone on the table and looked at it. "Six phone calls," he said. "I was asleep." He ran his hand through his hair. "They won't find the Thunderbird, but is there anything else there? Anything Dad left? You're sure?"

"I'm sure," I said. "Dex, it gets worse."

He looked at me, took in the dried blood on my face again, and he nodded. "Tell me."

So I told him. About Officer Kyle tailing me, pulling me over. About the fact that he was Tara's ex-fiancé. About how that made it personal for him. About how Officer Kyle knew I was a CI. Dex was the only person in the world I could talk to, because Dex already knew.

When I finished, Dex tossed the unlit joint and the lighter down on the table and scrubbed both his hands through his hair. "You think he meant it?" he said. "You think this cop will make the call?"

I pointed to my face. "He meant it," I said. "My guess is that Carter White is getting a phone call right now. If not from Officer Kyle, then from someone along the food chain. And he's being given my name."

Even Dex looked pale at that. Carter White was a big name in organized crime in Michigan: drugs, hookers, automatic weapons. There were rumors he'd bought half the politicians in the state, but even I hadn't found any evidence of that.

Still, I'd informed on plenty of Carter White's underlings in my career as a CI. He was the man Dad's entire stolen-car operation had reported to, and that was in ruins. I'd pulled the rug out from under a few of his other operations without being detected

—enough that he would be very interested in learning that the leak had been me.

Dex stared at me. His joint was forgotten on the table. "Jace, what are you going to do?"

"There isn't much I can do," I said. "If Officer Kyle has called me in, then I won't live past nightfall. It doesn't matter what I do or how far I run. He has an entire network that can find me. If Carter White wants me dead, it doesn't matter if it happens six hours from now, or ten, or twenty. In the end, I am fucking dead."

Fuck. It was hard to think about. Life hadn't been easy for me, but there were a lot of good things along the way. I'd met some good people—a few—and I'd read some good books. I had half a shot at connecting with my brothers for the first time in my life.

But it was Tara that made it hurt. She was the best thing that had ever happened to me. The best thing that could possibly ever happen to me. And for a short time, she had really been mine. Her courage and her relentless curiosity and her perfect skin and her sexy body. She had been all mine.

What do you want, Riggs?

All my life, I'd never taken the time to ask myself that question. I wanted to survive my childhood. I wanted enough money to pay the bills. I wanted someone to talk to. I wanted another good book to read. I wanted to get justice for my worthless father. I wanted to be good at something. I wanted to get out of prison. I wanted to be left alone.

I wanted Tara.

I *wanted* her. I wanted to be wherever she was. I wanted to know every piece of her. I wanted to drive her crazy and make her laugh and exasperate her. I wanted to fuck her and claim her and be the only man she ever looked at ever again.

I had never wanted anything like I wanted Tara Montgomery. Like I had from the first minute she looked at me from across that desk.

What do you want, Riggs?

"Jace," Dex said.

I looked at him. "Dex, do you remember the time I asked Dad for a bike when I was seven?"

Dex rubbed his ear, a gesture he didn't even know he was making, and I knew the answer before he spoke. "I remember it," he said, his voice flat. "I remember everything. Every time he hit me, called me a loser or a retard. I remember every time he called us names and every time he got drunk and forgot about us and every time he laughed at us. I remember every fucking thing."

"I wanted to get revenge on him," I said. "That's why I did what I did. But there was something else I always wanted. Something maybe I want even more. I wanted to do better than him. Be better than him."

My oldest brother looked, for the first time I could remember in a long time, dead sober and entirely sane. "Why are you here?" he asked me. "Of all the places you could have gone. Why did you come to my apartment?"

"Because you're the only one who can help me," I told him.

"Me?" he said. "You think I can actually help you out of this?"

"Of course you can," I said. "Did you think I was just going to lie down and die? I have a plan, dipshit."

He looked surprised, and then his eyes got that Dex gleam in them that I knew so well. "That sounds dangerous."

"It is. We could both get killed." I thought over the outcomes. "Or we could go to jail. But prison isn't so bad. I'll give you some tips. You just have to put up with a lot of jokes about dropping the soap."

My brother grinned.

"Tell me," he said. "I'm in."

TWENTY-SEVEN

Tara

"I'M FINE," Luke said. "The cops have sweated me before, Em. It's no big deal."

"Are you kidding me?" Emily said, her voice high in exasperation. "They interviewed you for *three hours*."

Luke cracked a beer open and shrugged. "Your mother sweated me in that same interview room a few months ago," he said. "Or don't you remember?"

"Luke, they *raided* the *shop*."

"Which your mother did a few months ago, too." Luke took a long swig of his beer. He looked a little tired, and he was drinking a beer at one in the afternoon, but he genuinely wasn't worried. "I'm a Riggs. I'm used to cops assuming I'm up to something."

We were in the kitchen of the Riggs house. Like the outside of the house, the inside showed a place that had long been neglected but was starting to get some attention. The cups were mismatched, but the floor and counters were clean. There was a stack of mail on the table, but there was also a tray with a hand-labeled sticker: *Important Bills!!!* It wasn't perfect, but someone cared, I could tell.

Emily was pacing the linoleum, freaking out. I gathered that Emily wasn't the quiet, stoic type. She was wearing jeans and a snug Tigers T-shirt that showed the shape of her breasts, a visual that Luke was obviously watching as he sipped his beer.

"Except you *were* up to something," Emily said. "You burned that stupid car."

Luke snorted. "The Thunderbird is nothing. So a few cars caught fire in Casey's junkyard, so what? Casey didn't see a damned thing."

Sitting at the kitchen table, I felt my stomach turn again. I thought I might throw up. Luke had told me the story about finding the coke, about getting rid of it. Jace must have been sick with worry when he found it, but he'd never let on to me. Of course he hadn't, because Jace was used to facing everything alone. Whether it was informing on his father's dirty business or finding coke stashed in the first car he got after getting out of prison. *Jesus, Jace, what must you have been feeling? Why didn't you tell me?*

I had texted Jace ten times, twenty. Called over and over. His phone was off.

It was probably for the best that he hadn't told me about the problems he was having. It was my ex-boyfriend, after all, who was determined to see him arrested or dead.

It's easier if they just go, Kyle had said. *So we arranged some encouragement.*

I said, "It was a setup. The whole coke thing. The drugs were planted by the Westlake PD."

"You're fucking right they were," Luke said. "I figured that out as soon as they got me in the station. We were idiots not to figure it out sooner."

Emily glared at Luke. "You're saying that my mother had cocaine planted in Jace's car? I swear to God, you are never getting laid again."

"No," Luke said calmly. Emily's freak-out seemed to be having no effect on him, like it was an everyday thing. "Nora wouldn't do that, but she isn't the only cop on the force. The cops always despised Dad, and the rest of us by default. Your mother felt the same until she sweated me last time and found out that I'm not so bad."

"That's just a theory!" Emily cried.

"It isn't a theory," I said. "My ex practically admitted it. He probably told Jace the same thing when he pulled him over. Which means that Jace knows that the Westlake PD is after him along with the criminals he informed on for all those years." I looked down at the table, my gaze taking nothing in. "This is all my fault. All of it."

Luke put his beer down and looked at me. "It wouldn't have mattered," he said.

"What?" I asked.

"If you'd told Jace about Officer Fuckface. It wouldn't have mattered to him." He shook his head. "I may have been away for eight years, but I know Jace. He's quiet but he's fierce. When he's set on something, he's fucking set on it, come hell or high water. And he's never been set on a woman the way he's set on you."

You don't know the half of it, I thought. *He never had a woman at all before me.* But that was Jace's business, and the last thing I was going to do was spill it to his brothers. "It's stupid," I said. "I should have warned him. But I was terrified I would lose him."

"You wouldn't have lost him," Luke said. "Not Jace."

"Well, I've lost him now," I said, still sick to my stomach.

Luke looked thoughtful. "I doubt it." A ringtone rang out, and all three of us tensed. It was Luke's phone. "Ryan," he said when he looked at the number. Then he answered. "What's up?"

There was a minute of talking on the other end. "No," Luke said. Then, "No. Oh, really?" He sighed. "Well, shit. I should have guessed. Got it. Bye." He hung up. "Ryan doesn't know where Jace is either, but guess who isn't answering his fucking phone? Our oldest brother, Dexter Riggs."

Emily had stopped pacing. "Dex?" she said. "Jace went to see Dex?"

I straightened. "What?" I asked them. "What does that mean?" I didn't know Dex. I didn't know Ryan, either. But Luke and Emily looked genuinely alarmed. "Is there something wrong with Dex?"

"That's a complicated question," Emily said.

"Yes," Luke said. "Dex is crazy."

"He's also in Detroit," Emily said. "Or at least, he's supposed to be."

I opened my mouth to say something. I didn't know what. Maybe to say that Jace wasn't with Dex. That Jace had possibly just gone into hiding. He was smart and sensible, and the Riggs brothers weren't close. Jace wouldn't take this into his own hands and do anything crazy. That wasn't his way.

Then my phone pinged with a text, and I read it. It was Jace. He must have turned his phone on.

Tell me something true, he wrote.

Everything went away. The house, Luke and Emily, the world around me. There was just him and me.

I didn't even hesitate. I typed, *You're beautiful.*

There was a second's pause, then the dots moved. *Tara. I'm not.*

You don't see what I see, I wrote. *It's the truth. Your turn.*

You stole mine, Jace, wrote, *but I'll try again. The reason I picked a fight with you in our first session was because I knew I couldn't have you, and I couldn't stand it. So I was a jerk. If you hated me, I thought it would be easier. It was the only thing I could think of to do.*

My throat was thick. The words themselves were pure Jace, but I felt panic rising in my chest. *It didn't work,* I wrote. *I woke up the next morning having a sex dream about you.*

Another pause, and the dots moved again. *I didn't know that,* Jace wrote. *I like it.*

Why does this sound so strangely final?

Is it? Jace wrote. *I don't want it to be.*

Come back, I wrote. *We'll figure this out. We'll figure everything out. In case you hadn't clued in, I'm in love with you.*

I don't deserve that, but I'll take it. And I'm trying my best to come back. But I have to turn my phone off now.

"No," I said out loud. I typed furiously. *Don't you dare. CALL ME.*

But he was already gone, I knew it.

I looked up and saw Luke and Emily watching me. How long had they been standing there? What had they seen, what had they said that I hadn't heard? I had no idea.

"He's doing something crazy," I said to them, my voice cracking. "We have to go to Detroit."

TWENTY-EIGHT

Jace

IT WAS some kind of poetic justice that Carter White met me at one of his chop shops. It was a warehouse on the outskirts of Detroit, in one of the many industrial parks that were only semi-occupied. It was five o'clock in the morning, and except for a restless hour of semi-sleep plagued by nightmares, I'd been awake for nearly twenty-four hours. I was simultaneously exhausted and floating, my head as light as if it were detached from my body, my eyes stinging, my feelings numb.

I got out of Emily's Tercel in the empty parking lot and walked to the back door, as I'd been instructed. I knocked twice and the door opened, revealing a big heavy guy in a suit. He carried a Glock in one hand as easily as if it were tissue paper. "Get in," he said.

Inside were two other guys, equally big and equally armed. They patted me down, looking for weapons or wires, and found nothing. They took my phone, saw that it was powered off, and one of them put it in his pocket. Then they took me to the main warehouse, sat me on a chair in front of a table, and stood behind each shoulder. Neither of them spoke.

It was a huge space, dimly lit. This was one of White's workshops, where stolen cars were brought to be made over and resold. It was as familiar to me as my own hands. I could smell metal and motor oil, that tangy smell I knew so well. I'd always thought I'd like to die smelling that smell, and I realized now that I might get my wish. I kept my face a blank and waited.

He made me wait, of course. Men as important as Carter White didn't just show up to any old meeting, even the ones that they'd called. Maybe someone was checking me out through a camera somewhere; I had no idea. It was tempting to fidget, but I'd done a lot of waiting in my life, and a little more wasn't going to kill me. I sat still with a silent man behind each of my shoulders and thought about nothing.

Eventually, a slim man in a well-cut suit came around the corner. He, too, carried a Glock. He did so elegantly, easily, as if he carried one all the time. He pulled out a chair and sat across from me, still holding the gun.

"Jace Riggs," he said.

"Yes," I replied.

He wasn't a bad-looking guy. He was white, his face a little narrow, his nose a little big. He looked at me with eyes like dark stones, flat and hard.

"I'm surprised you showed up," he said. "You know I called you here to kill you."

I did know that. I knew the minute my phone rang with an unknown number and a disguised voice on the other end told me where to go. I'd informed on men like Carter White long enough to know they didn't fuck around. "Was there any point in running?" I asked.

He smiled briefly, humorlessly. "No. Of course not. Still, most people don't walk into their own death."

I glanced at the Glock he held in his lap, gleaming and silent. I had no doubt it was loaded, the safety off. Carter White was known for making people disappear, never to be seen again. It would take a split second to kill me, and then what? Did he have somewhere to put my body? He must have a concrete pit or something. If I knew where that pit was, I'd have told the authorities about it. Now I was likely going to end up in it.

"You could have had one of your guys do it," I said to Carter. "When you called me to a meeting, I figured you want to talk. Maybe there's something that will get me out of this."

"There isn't," Carter said, and when his eyes gleamed I realized that beneath those flat stones he was angry. Very, very angry. "You've cost me a great deal, Riggs. I've had operations shut down and moved. I've had associates arrested. I've had to pay a fortune to lawyers and to make certain people stay quiet. You've wasted my money and my time, and today I learned that you were just a low-level car thief. Just some idiot, the son of the idiot who ran the Westlake operation." He shook his head. "I thought someone had it out for you, but the fact that you came here tonight proves it's true."

"I wasn't going to convince you otherwise," I said. "I got nailed by a cop because I fell for his ex-girlfriend."

"I hope she was worth it."

"She was. What do you want to know?"

"The truth," Carter said. "I want to know who hired you to do what you did."

"No one hired me," I said, which was true.

"Bullshit," Carter said. "You have nothing to lose anymore, Riggs. If Alfonso hired you, tell me now."

"I don't know who that is," I said. Also true—I had no fucking idea what he was talking about.

But Carter leaned forward, never taking his hand from the gun lying on his lap. "Listen to me, you piece of shit," he said in a low, furious voice. "Alfonso isn't going to cover for you. He isn't going to save you. He's going to let you go to the dogs. You have no reason to be loyal. Tell me the truth, and I might make this quick."

Cold sweat started on the back of my neck. I didn't know any Alfonso, had never heard of him. This wasn't how I'd thought this would go. I'd thought that Carter would ask me questions I could actually answer so I could buy time. I had to buy time.

"I've been inside for twenty months," I said. "I'm not in the game anymore. I don't know who Alfonso is, and he sure as shit didn't hire me. I did what I did because I hate my father. For free."

For a second—just a second—I thought I'd convinced him. Then Carter lifted a finger, and one of his goons grabbed each of my arms. Before I could move, they'd handcuffed each of my wrists to metal rings that were sunk into the table. I jerked my arms, looked down, and saw that the table was cemented to the floor.

No, this was definitely *not* how this was supposed to go.

Carter gave another signal, and I heard a rustling behind me. I looked over my shoulder to see that one of the goons was laying down plastic sheeting on the floor.

"Jesus, Carter," I said. "You don't have to do this. I don't know who Alfonso is."

"Yes, you do," Carter said, standing up. He came around the table, the gun in his hand. "Do you want to know something interesting? A percentage of those who try to blow their brains out don't succeed. They blow part of their skull off instead." He touched the gun to my jaw. "Some of them just blow off a section of their jawbone and the bullet doesn't hit the brain at all. Others rip out the backs of their throats. It's an extraordinarily painful experience. And in the end, they don't even die." He paused. "I think I'll experiment."

I went very still. I didn't have much choice, but from the angle of my head I also had a view of Carter's wrist. He was wearing a watch.

It was 5:17. I let my breath saw in and out of my lungs as I watched the tiny gold second hand sweep around the watch's face. This hadn't gone according to plan, but I just needed five more seconds in which Carter White didn't pull the trigger. Five more seconds in which he didn't blow half of my face off in the most painful way possible.

What do you want, Riggs?

I just want five more seconds. To save my life.

Four. Three, two...

Carter aimed the gun.

Tara, I thought.

Then I threw myself forward as the first shots started and the SWAT team broke in.

TWENTY-NINE

Jace

FOUR HOURS later I was still sitting in a hospital room. I hadn't been hurt in Carter White's chop shop, but they checked me out anyway. A nurse cleaned the cut Officer Kyle had given me on my temple and put a stitch in it. They examined the bruise on my right wrist, where I'd wrenched it in the handcuffs, ducking away from Carter.

Doctors questioned me, and then cops. More cops. Detroit cops, then plainclothes cops who were obviously higher rank. Then Westlake cops, and then Westlake plainclothes cops. A lawyer came in with his own questions and went away again. Then another doctor, and yet another plainclothes cop. I told them all whatever they wanted.

The worst thing was that they'd taken away my phone. They had to, because my phone had recorded the entire conversation. It had only looked like it was turned off—in fact Dex had installed an app that made your phone look off when in fact it was on. It was probably mostly used by students in class and people in meetings, but today I'd used it to record Carter White threatening to kill me. Actually one of Carter's suited guys had recorded it, because he'd put my phone in his breast pocket and stood there, unaware that he was a microphone broadcasting the entire conversation to the SWAT team closing in.

So they needed my phone for the recording. Still, that left me with no way to call Tara, no way to call my brothers and tell them I was okay. They wouldn't let me leave, and no one was allowed into the hospital room that became my makeshift interrogation room.

I was sitting on the edge of the bed, fully dressed, thinking about just walking out and letting the cops catch me later when the door opened and Dex walked in.

"Jesus, they let you past the guards," I said.

"Ha ha," Dex said. He was wearing his disintegrating jeans and an old Redwings shirt so faded it wasn't red anymore. "I heard the recording. Jesus. That was pretty fucking close."

I stood up. It was Dex who had called his old contacts on the force to set up the sting. The cops wanted Carter White, and Carter White wanted me. So when I agreed to meet Carter, the cops came along in a couple of unmarked vans—courtesy of Dex—and gave me eighteen minutes to get in place in the chop shop. Then they got the most prestigious arrest of the year, and Dex did some repair on his tarnished reputation. Everyone was happy, except me, because I'd be hearing the sound of plastic being laid out behind me until the end of my fucking life.

Jesus, I was tired. I couldn't remember anymore when I'd last slept. Or ate. The only option here was chips from the vending machine, and just the thought of it made me feel nauseated. A lot of things made me feel nauseated.

"We done?" I said to Dex. "I'm leaving."

Dex looked concerned. "Where are you going?"

I had to put my thoughts together to answer. "To Tara's. I have to talk to her, tell her I'm okay."

"You're going all the way back to Westlake?"

"Where else am I supposed to go?"

"Jace," Dex said, "you don't have a car. The last I saw, it was still parked at that warehouse. And you're in no shape to do the drive."

"I'll figure something out. And I'm fine."

He sighed. "And you don't have to go back to Westlake to find Tara. She's downstairs in the lobby with Luke and Emily, waiting for them to release you."

I stared at him. Here? Tara was *here*? While I'd spent hours wondering how to get access to a fucking phone? The thought made me angry, then tired again. I had to get the hell out of here.

"Thanks for the SWAT team, Dex," I said. "They were handy. Nice work. See you later."

He moved to block me at the door. "Have you been released to go?"

"I don't care," I said. "If they want me, they know where I live. They'll have to come in person, because I no longer have a phone. But I'm telling you, I'm gone."

He looked at my face for a second and gave in. "Okay, I'll take care of it. They're downstairs. Just go."

THERE WERE TOO many people at the hospital. In the corridors, in the elevator, too many faces moving too fast. It was hard to scan them all, looking for Tara.

I wandered around the lobby, over to the ER entrance, back to another entrance that was an MRI room. No Luke, no Emily, no Tara. No one paid me any mind, even with the small bandage on my temple—I was just another patient, albeit a dressed one. In the end I stood in the middle of the large open space of the lobby, turning slowly in a circle, looking for that distinctive fall of dark brown hair.

She was in line at a small kiosk that sold coffee. I recognized her hair, her long legs in dark jeans. When I circled beside her and touched her elbow, she turned and gasped.

"Jace," she said. She left the line, grabbed my arm, dragged me away. Then she flung her arms around me.

She smelled like shampoo and hospital hand soap and Tara. She was wearing a soft gray zip-up sweatshirt I'd never seen before, and I pressed my face into it. She held me so tight she nearly cracked something in my neck, and her hands were in my hair. She was saying something, but she was half sobbing so I couldn't hear it.

I held her back, my arms around her waist, holding on. Just holding on.

"They took my phone," I told her. "Sorry."

She loosened her grip a little and leaned back, looking at me. "What?"

"I couldn't call you." There was something else I was supposed to say. "I don't have Emily's car either, so I can't give it back to her. It's parked in a lot somewhere."

"It's okay," Tara said. She wasn't wearing any makeup, and her face was a little pale. She must have been worried. How long was she worried?

"I had to turn my phone off," I said. "To use the app. It wasn't because I didn't want to talk to you."

She put her hands on my face, her palms cradling my jaw. "Baby, how long has it been since you slept?"

"Your place. It's made me a little stupid, sorry."

"You're never stupid," she said softly. She gently touched my bandage. "This is all my fault."

"Don't say that ever again," I told her.

But she only frowned. "He's off the force," she said, brushing her thumb over my cheekbone like she couldn't quite stop touching me. Like she was memorizing me. I watched her beautiful mouth and realized I'd forgotten to kiss it. "He's gone. You can file a complaint, you know. Police brutality. It's all on his dashboard camera."

"No," I said. "I'm never having anything to do with cops again."

She nodded, her gaze softening as she looked at me. "Are you hurt, Jace? Tell me the truth."

"I'm not hurt," I said. "It was bad, though. I might need therapy."

I meant it in my tired brain as a joke, but her expression grew tight. Always so serious about helping people, my Tara. "I can find you someone. Someone good. You need to tell me if you're having any symptoms—nightmares, insomnia, anxiety attacks. That sort of thing."

"That sounds like my everyday life," I said. I was joking again, but she got even more serious if that was possible, so I said, "Never mind. You're going to know whether I have symptoms because you're coming home with me and you're not leaving."

She blinked at me, and then she smiled, just a little. I lived for that smile. "Okay."

"We don't have to have sex unless you want to, but I have to say I'm going to be hoping pretty fucking hard."

The smile got wider. "I like you, sleep-deprived Jace. You're sweet."

"I'm always sweet," I said, touching her hair. There had been a moment when I thought I'd never touch her hair again. "The main reason I'm pissed they took my phone is because it has the text on it where you say you're in love with me."

She blinked hard, and I thought maybe there were tears in her eyes, but that couldn't be right. "I am in love with you," she said. "Now kiss me, and we'll go find Luke and Emily and go home."

THIRTY

Tara

JACE SLEPT on the drive home. We were in Luke's Charger, a car I hadn't confessed to Luke that I'd made out with his brother in. I'd mention that probably never. Luke was driving, Emily was up front, and Jace and I were in the back. Almost immediately Jace lay down with his head in my lap. He looked almost comical because he was so big; his legs were folded like an ironing board in a closet. I stroked his hair, he mumbled something that sounded like *I'm crashing,* and then he was asleep.

"Shit, his feet are on my upholstery," Luke said. Emily punched his arm. It was the last thing any of us said on the drive.

I was exhausted myself. We'd gone back and forth from Westlake to Detroit and back, trying to track down Jace or Dex, searching for news. I'd been home long enough to change my clothes and get a few hours' sleep before Dex called and told us what had happened, and we'd been back on the road to Detroit again. I felt like I had been living in Luke's car and the hospital for weeks.

My fault, the voice in my head piped up again. *My fault.*

The logical part of me knew it wasn't. It was Kyle's fault this had happened—he had tried to get Jace killed. I didn't know why; it wasn't because Kyle loved me or even cared all that much. *Housekeeping,* he'd called it. How had I been with a man who could sentence another man to death and call it housekeeping? How had I lived with him, kissed him, slept with him, nearly married him? How had I not known he was a cop who could stoop so low? I was supposed to be the expert on other people, but what a joke that was. I knew nothing at all.

So, yes, it was my fault. It was my fault that I'd ever gone on a date with Kyle in the first place. It was my fault I'd fallen, even a little, for his bullshit when I was supposed to know better. When it was my job to see through people's bullshit every day. I'd thought that Kyle was the kind of guy I was supposed to be with, and I'd let that idea make my life choices, and Jace had almost died for it.

So I owed Jace Riggs. Again. He had trusted me with everything—literally everything, including the fact that he was sleeping in my lap right now. He was still trusting me. I would have to make it up to him.

When we got back to the Riggs house, I said a tired goodnight to Luke and Emily and led a groggy Jace into the guest house. We managed to get our shoes off before we both fell on the bed and slept.

WHEN I WOKE up it was raining outside. The clock said it was eleven o'clock at night—what night? I didn't remember what day of the week it was, and I didn't care. Jace was still beside me, deep asleep.

You're coming home with me and you're not leaving, he'd said. I was fine with that. I'd go back to my place in the morning just long enough to pick up some things; I didn't feel like being anywhere but here. I walked into his tiny kitchen and found a can of soup, which I heated over the stove element. I ate some of it, leaving the rest for Jace when he woke up, and drank some water. Then I stripped my clothes off and stepped into the shower.

The hot water was heaven. Jace didn't have any girly soaps or shampoos, but I made do. I was just rinsing when I heard the bathroom door open.

I hadn't locked it. I didn't see the point. I looked over my shoulder through the glass and saw the blurry, steamy figure of a huge, naked, bearded man. Then the shower door opened and Jace got in with me.

It was a close fit; it wasn't a big shower. I turned to find myself up against his chest, the fine layer of soft hair brushing my nipples. The water rippled down the muscles of his shoulders and his amazing stomach. His cock was halfway hard and getting harder.

I looked up at his face. He was looking down at me, his gaze unreadable.

So I asked him the first thing that came into my mind, which was, "Do you want to talk?"

Jace's gaze never wavered. "No," he said, those dark gray eyes sucking me in like they had from the first moment I'd seen them. "I don't want to talk." Then he leaned in and kissed me.

I'd been so worried, so torn apart, so lost inside my own head. For a second my heart leaped and my chest contracted because I'd forgotten the feel of him, the reality of Jace, of this man and his big body that was made for mine.

But as always he started a fire, and I felt my body burn as I pressed up against him. It felt like a year since we'd done this, since I'd felt his hands twist in my hair and cup my head as he kissed me deeper and deeper. We were *supposed* to do this, him and me. I opened my mouth and slid my hand down through the hot water, taking his cock and giving it a long stroke. Jace made a sound deep in his throat that made me throb. I'd never get tired of that sound as long as I lived.

He was hot and hard and I wanted to keep stroking, make him make that sound again, but he broke the kiss and ran his hands down to my breasts, stroking them. Then he put his hands on the curve of my waist as he sank to his knees.

I inhaled and leaned my head back under the water. We hadn't done this standing up yet, but oh my god, he was so good at it. He leaned in and parted my pussy, licking gently inside me, tasting and rubbing me. I moaned and tried to keep my balance with my hands on the wet shower tiles. He slid two fingers inside me and stroked me as he licked my clit and I felt it through my whole body, pleasure licking up through my spine and down to my feet, my nipples going hard under the hot water, my legs trying to part wider.

Still, he was merciless. He kept his fingers inside me and closed his mouth over me, pressing in just the right spot. I moaned as my hips bucked, out of my control. There had never been anyone who could make me feel like this. He'd been in the shower with me for mere minutes, and already I was close to coming, my legs shaking and my body on fire. His firm hands held me still so I wouldn't fall, but also trapping me so I could do nothing but accept pleasure. I could do nothing but surrender and feel.

I broke apart hard, the orgasm sharp as a knife. It felt overdue, like I hadn't come in years despite the fact that Jace had given me a string of orgasms a few nights ago. I cried out, the sound echoing in the shower as I pressed against his talented mouth.

Jace stood up. For a second he cupped me possessively, his beard scraping my neck as he kissed me there. Then he turned the shower off and we moved to the bed.

He'd been slow with me before, but not now. Now he turned me on my stomach and pushed my legs apart, putting his knees between mine. He held himself over my back and kissed the back of my shoulder, the back of my neck. "Fuck, I need you," he said, his voice tight with restraint.

"Yes," I said.

His hands moved to my hips again. He lifted them up and in one motion he thrust inside me all the way, a stab of sensation that made me cry out in pleasure. He pulled out and thrust in again as my hands curled in the sheets, gripped the edge of the pillow. He braced himself over me, one hand on the bed with the other still on my hip, and thrust into me again. I dropped my head, my hair falling over the pillow as I closed my eyes and did nothing but feel.

We fit like this. So perfectly I just held myself and let him take me, over and over. There was an edge to the way he fucked me, desperation, like he'd thought he'd never do it again. I let him do what he wanted, how he wanted, because it felt so good I never wanted him to stop. I wanted to feel his hand on my hip and his breath on the back of my neck and his knees between mine. It was heaven.

"Fuck, you're perfect," he said in my ear. "I want to be inside you all the fucking time."

"Yes," I said, because that was all I could think of to say. *Yes, yes, yes, yes.* "Fuck me harder."

He made a low, turned-on sound and slammed into me harder as we rocked the bed. He was big, and it was harsh, and it made me ache in the best way. I moved a hand down between my legs and stroked myself, feeling myself climb again. I had no shame. I came again, my hips bucking up against his heavy weight, my pussy squeezing him over and over.

"Jesus Christ, Tara," Jace said, and then he came long and hard inside me as we finally slowed down. We were out of breath and sweating, still wet from the shower. Jace pulled out of me and lay next to me and we both stared at the ceiling, panting.

"Was I too rough?" he asked me after a minute.

"God, no," I said. "I liked it."

He rolled over and propped himself up on an elbow, looking down at me. He searched my face for a second, making sure I was telling the truth. "I really fucking love you," he said, his voice gruff.

I laughed, because it was such a Jace thing to say, and because hearing him say it gave me a burst of pure joy. "I love you too," I said.

He traced a fingertip along my jaw. "You really think we can make this work?"

"I have no idea," I said, thinking of the advice Catherine had given me, "but you aren't getting rid of me. If you try and dump me, I'll get you back. As many times as it takes."

He shook his head, his gray eyes thoughtful. "All right, then. If you're in, so am I."

I was in. I didn't know the future. I didn't know if we would work out. I didn't know where we would live, what we would do. I didn't know if we would get married or have kids. I didn't know if my parents would like him or if his brothers would like me. And I was okay with all of it.

I didn't know much, but I knew Jace. So I pulled him down to me and kissed him.

It seemed like the best thing I could do.

THIRTY-ONE

Jace

Four months later

WHEN TARA GOT home from work, I was on the couch, reading. I had my head on one arm of the couch and my feet over the other. I lowered my book and watched her come through the door.

She kicked off her shoes—she always did that first—and then dropped her purse, exhaling a breath. "Hey," she said to me. "What's for dinner?"

I raised my eyebrows at her. "Takeout is on the counter." She had worked late, which meant that dinner was my job. Except I couldn't cook to save my life. As if she would be surprised.

She walked to the counter, checked out what I'd bought, nodded in approval. "Okay." Then she bypassed the food and opened the fridge to pull out her go-to bottle of white wine. "First things first."

"That good a day?" I asked.

She shrugged. "Just long." But there was a knot of a frown between her eyebrows, and her expression was distracted as she poured her wine.

We were in our apartment—our place. An apartment we'd rented together. I was still in shock, to tell the truth, that I was actually living with her. We'd moved in a month ago, and so far I hadn't fucked it up, which was incredible. I told myself that if Tara came to her senses and kicked me out, I could always pack a bag and go back to the guest house.

Then I'd try and get her back. As many times as it took.

I watched as Tara sipped her wine, then unzipped her slim black pants and pulled them off. It was a nice show, but I knew it wasn't for me. She was stressed out about something, and she was trying to get comfortable. Wearing just her work blouse and her panties, she picked up her wine again and came my way.

"What are you reading?" she asked.

She would tell me what was wrong sooner or later. I could wait. "*Jane Eyre,*" I said, showing her the cover. "Just like you told me to."

That made her smile. "You needed to read something besides that godawful Dostoevsky. What do you think?"

I frowned. "She's thinking about marrying that St. John guy, which would be a big fucking mistake. She doesn't belong with him at all."

Tara approached the couch and swung one long, bare leg over me, lowering herself onto my lap, straddling me while still holding her wine. "She's trying to figure out how to be a good person," she said.

I was lost for a second, because I was looking at those long legs, but then I remembered what we were talking about. "She doesn't need to marry a prig and go be a religious bore to be a good person," I said. "She can be a good person by being with Rochester and helping with his fucked-up self."

"Well, I won't give it away," Tara said, smiling at me. She took a sip of her wine, and then her brow knotted again. "I just learned that one of my clients went back to prison."

I frowned at her. "Not your fault," I said. "You know that, right?"

"Logically, yes," Tara said. She was comfortable now, sitting on my lap like she belonged there. I wasn't about to move. She swallowed and looked away. "I mean, I do know that. And it's happened before. But it always makes me think about what I could be doing better."

"You can't save everyone in the world," I told her. I took her free hand and kissed the back of it. "You do good work. Just look at me."

I'd always be an ex-con, but I was a respectable businessman now. Sort of. We had opened a second location of Riggs Auto, this one on the right side of the tracks, in the nicer part of town. Ryan had moved back to Westlake with his son, and we made it look like the new location was Ryan's, which gave it a steady stream of customers. Behind the scenes, I did most of the books, the planning, and the marketing. Ryan just fixed the cars, sometimes shirtless. It was a license to print money.

"That's different," Tara said.

"No, it isn't." I let her hand go. "Something else is bugging you. What is it?"

She sighed. "They want to give me a promotion at work."

I felt my eyebrows go up. "You don't sound enthused."

"It would be more of an administrative role," she said, sipping her wine again. "I'd be doing more back-end work, going to meetings and looking at budgets. I wouldn't be seeing so many clients face to face. It's a pay raise, but I feel like I won't be helping as many people as I could."

I thought about that. She was always so hard on herself, my Tara. Always looking for ways she could be improving herself, doing a better job than she already was. The truth was she could do just about anything she set her mind to. "If you're looking at budgets, then you're deciding how the money is spent," I said.

"True."

"So you could decide to hire more counselors, or better ones, or improve the kind of counseling they do. You could decide to take on more clients who need it but can't afford it. You could spend some of that money on Saturday hours for people who work all week and can't afford to take a day off."

Tara looked at me, the frown between her eyes.

"You could improve the outreach," I said. "You could, say, offer sessions to abused women or abused kids. Get some specialists in to teach your counselors what to do. Organize talks at schools. Connect up with the cops and emergency services for women who need restraining orders." I shrugged. "Okay, I don't really know what I'm talking about. But you see what I mean."

"Jesus, Jace," Tara said. "How do you do it?"

"Do what?"

"Make everything make so much *sense.* It's like your superpower. I've been conflicted about this all day."

"I don't see why. You can do lots of good as an administrator. More, maybe."

She sighed. "Obviously, I should listen to you about everything."

"Really?" I smiled at her. "Okay, take your panties off."

She smiled back. "Nuh-uh," she said, putting her glass of wine down. "I'm starving. Dinner first." She leaned forward and kissed me, and I cupped her head, made it go on longer. She tasted like wine, and I licked it from her mouth, making her groan.

"Trying again," I said when I broke the kiss. "Take your panties off."

"Not yet," she said. "Later."

But she leaned in and kissed me again, and this time was deeper.

I had her.

And it was the only thing I wanted.

ALSO BY JULIE KRISS

The Riggs Brothers Series

Drive Me Wild

Take Me Down

Work Me Up (Coming Soon)

Make Me Beg (Coming Soon)

The Bad Billionaire Series

Bad Billionaire

Dirty Sweet Wild

Rich Dirty Dangerous

Back in Black

Standalone

Spite Club

The Eden Hills Duet

Bad Boyfriend

Bad Wedding

The King Family Series

The Bastard (Coming Soon)

38751715R00111

Printed in Great Britain
by Amazon